T0209338

A Unicorn of Kkhadee
*The Invasion of Peasant-Earth
The Milky Galaxy
Pools of Thought
The Golden Son

THE RABBLE AND THE RICH SERIES:
(the story in each book is complete and can stand alone)

The Butterfly Caper
The Secret Experiment
Learning to Share
Inherit the Earth

THE
INVASION
OF
PEASANT-EARTH

THE INVASION OF PEASANT-EARTH

iUniverse books may be ordered through booksellers or by contacting:

iUniverse
1663 Liberty Drive
Bloomington, IN 47403
www.iuniverse.com
844-349-9409

ISBN: 978-1-6632-2608-2 (sc)
ISBN: 978-1-6632-2609-9 (e)

Library of Congress Control Number: 2021916988

Print information available on the last page.

iUniverse rev. date: 08/31/2021

for
Kathryn Wilhelm

"Hard times are coming when we will be wanting the voices of writers who can see alternatives to how we live now and can see through *our fear stricken society* and *its obsessive technologies* to other ways of being, and even imagine some real grounds for hope."

~ Ursula K. LeGuin, 2014
in her acceptance speech
upon receiving **the Distinguished Contribution to American Letters Medal**,
of the **National Book Awards**

PROLOGUE

─────── ▼ ───────

THE INVADERS

The huge starship had been decelerating at 1.7G for several light-months until its speed was finally manageable on a planetary scale. As it approached Earth, prior to inserting itself into a high orbit, it did not destroy or disturb the communications satellites swarming around the planet— so as not to alert the Earthers to the coming Invasion.

▼

Tom Worthington woke from cryo-sleep. Slowly, then quickly — jarringly — his REM dreams caused him to try and turn over and he found he couldn't because he was tied down! And cold! In a coffin! He started to yell and the lid was lifted. He choked the scream back in his throat and stared at the face above him.

"Private Worthington, I presume?" the man said, grinning. There were sergeant stripes on his sleeve.

Tom gritted his teeth and snarled, twisting in his confinement. He was beginning to remember: *his cat Dinger purring, the campus, mutated Elm trees, walking, in the shade, to his classroom, standing at the lectern* . . .

"Go ahead and piss," the Sergeant said as he started to release Tom. "You're hooked up. Ah! That's it. You're filling the bag." He threw off the binding tapes. "All right, out of the box. Here —" He clamped the fill tube as Tom, naked, leaned over the side of the cryo-box and fell out onto the cold floor.

Tom clambered slowly to his feet, fighting a sudden sensation of nausea and vertigo, clutching the sergeant's arm. His legs trembled and his eyesight was blurred.

"Take your bag, down that-a-way, to the recycle," the Sergeant snapped. "On the bounce! We're in Earth orbit. Squad meeting."

▼

Tom walked slowly, still unsteady on his feet and sick to his oh-so-empty! stomach.

He remembered now. He had been Professor Thomas Andrew Worthington, a PhD in Anthropology, on a fast track to tenure. He had been lecturing at Clarke University in Rockefeller City, on the planet Faraday. He had recently been given permission by the Board of Reproduction to start incubating a clone-son.

Then he had been drafted, torn from his pleasant, contemplative, academic life. Trained and frozen. Because he was a young man.

Even though the round-trip from the star system of Delta Pavonis — 19.9 light years from Earth — at sub-light speeds would take over 200 years out and back in cold sleep, the men whose ideals controlled the planet Faraday were sufficiently desperate to gamble on invading Earth. Tiny probes had been sent on a round trip at near-light speed over forty years before. They had discovered that Earth's output of man-made electromagnetic radiation, and its number of artificial satellites, revealed Earth still held *at least* semi-tech human beings. The Faradayans believed that, properly dominated, the descendents of *the Losers — poor rural people and uncivilized wilderness dwellers —* those abandoned on Earth — could solve every crisis survival problem of Faraday's advanced human population.

Tom's ancestors had left Earth over fifteen centuries before.

▼

On his way back from the recycle, Tom passed several men carrying their urine bags to discard.

The Sergeant gave him a warm robe and hustled him into a group meeting of other recently-thawed men in their squad. Tom stood beside his best friend, Bill—William Richard McClevy, a PhD in Earth History, formerly a full professor at Clarke University—who, over 100 years before, had been drafted into the Invasion Army along with Tom. They had been frozen for the star trip with almost 400,000 other young men.

Like the rest of the men, including Tom himself, Bill looked miserable, with thick bags under his eyes and the muscles of his cheeks drooping like old rags. He was still shaking from the cold, his shoulders twitching irregularly. Tom stood close beside his friend, shoulder-to-shoulder, clumsily offering his support, reluctant like any heterosexual man to put his arm around his old friend, whom he loved dearly, giving him physical comfort.

"Ten hut!" the Sergeant snapped.

▼

Tom, Bill, and the other newly unfrozen soldiers in their squad—all of them fuzzy with post-cryo nausea—stood groggily in lines at attention as the sergeant paced back and forth lecturing them. The situation was familiar from the Basic Training they had endured before being cryo-frozen.

"Listen up!" the Sergeant shouted. "You all know what's at stake. Some of you care more than others" — he looked pointedly at Tom — "but right now, you all need to eat and recuperate, and then after some sexual recreation," he said, eyeing Tom's friend Bill, "we'll get together in the auditorium for a final briefing of the current situation. Then we'll be ready to go where the Colonels send us."

The Sergeant faced the squad, his hands on his hips. "The Invasion should be over in only a few days," he barked. "Not much real fighting. Those stupid, primitive Left-Behinds have *NO* defenses. They are unarmed! Can you imagine?" He threw up his hands. "Unarmed!

"As we understand it, they naively have a philosophy of world peace. They're total losers!"

1

▼

PEASANT-EARTH

On the Earth below, on the North American Continent, the brightening amber line of dawn swept across the flat Kansas landscape toward Yellowood Dairy Farm. It was on the road still called K-96, four miles east of the Village of Dighton. At the farm, a pleasant trill of first-bells sounded in the bedroom of the young farmer whose chore it was to feed the animals and help milk the cows before most of her fellow communards—except for those few whose task was cooking breakfast— also had to get out of bed.

Lizzy Alamota was a tall woman, 27 years old, blessed with tan-coloured skin and hazel-colored eyes protected by epicanthic folds. Tightly curled, dark reddish-gold hair crowned her head in a short cap. Smiling, she opened her eyes to the green-tinged sunlight across her bed. The sunny southern wall of her room — a large window and transparent door of strong glass — held a riot of living grape leaves weaving up around a sturdy wooden trellis. Lizzy lay on her back and stretched in the sunlight to work out her overnight kinks. A calico cat on the foot of her bed complained about being disturbed as Lizzy kicked off her bed sheet.

It was the beginning of a beautiful early spring day in the year 3683.

Lizzy bounced, bright-eyed, to the toilet-room to relieve herself. She shared that facility — which contained a bathtub, shower, sink, toilet, and bidet — with those communards currently sleeping in the bedroom on the other side of it. Lizzy was a morning-person, happy to awaken each day to the routine adventures of farming life, eager to greet each day as a gift. Her early-morning need for the toilet room never conflicted with the schedule of those communards sharing it. They were not morning people. They had waked only slightly at the sound of first-bells and had rolled over to return to the 'luxury' of 'sleeping-in' for another forty-five minutes until second-bells.

Sitting on the edge of her double bed and yawning in the predawn light, Lizzy drew on her work clothes: soft, well-worn canvas trousers, tall muckboots, and an old red T-shirt that said, front and back:

▼

**Lane County Fair
Alamota Village
3 legged race**

4

JULY 6, 3672

▼

Picking a ripe tomato to tide her over until breakfast, Lizzy exited the passive-solar farmhouse — an Earthship® — through the greenhouse corridor outside her bedroom. She walked several yards along a dirt path thickly carpeted with straw through a lush vegetable garden toward the barn. She was accompanied by a gaggle of excited cats, dogs, and phoxes (domesticated, descended from wild foxes) who knew she would soon feed them. Lizzy grinned at them. She had often thought, *There's no point in being a farmer if you don't like spending your life with animals.*

Eastward, past the neighboring fields, Earth's sun was just peeking over the straight edge of the world's horizon.

The thick-walled barn was clean, cool, and aromatic. Lizzy fed the Farm's six cows first so they would be disinclined to fuss while they were being milked. She patted them softly as she moved around the barn. As with everyone living and working at Yellowood Farm, she liked the mild-mannered, milk-filled Jersey-cows, who were her special bovine friends.

Crossing over to the other side of the double barn, she fed the horses the Yellowood farmers kept for recreational riding, local transportation, and production of organic fertilizer. Lizzy liked horses. She appreciated their quick, native intelligence in contrast to the placid, dim awareness of the dairy cows.

Dark-skinned Suzie, one of the Dighton 'twins,' her black, kinky hair all spiky and in disarray, arrived soon, tall muckboots on her feet, apparently still in her pajamas. "G'morning," she mumbled to Lizzy as she passed through the horse-half of the barn on her way to milk by-hand the farm's cows. At that time in history, most people involved in dairy farming believed mechanical milking alienated both the humans and the cows.

Milk bucket between her knees, Suzie began milking the docile cows, all newly freshened and attended by their hungry offspring. Calves were never denied access to the milk supply their births had generated.

Meanwhile, Lizzy fed the chickens mixed grains and shredded table scraps while they clucked around her in their little yard under the mulberry trees. Their enthusiastic, single-minded pecking always amused her. Then she fed the dogs and the phoxes their mixed omnivore diet, and only a little milk for the cats who would still enthusiastically stalk and eat mice.

Long ago it had been discovered that mice and voles—as well as chipmunks and squirrels—could not be removed, without serious ecological consequences, from the Earth's natural ecosystem. Their numbers were still best controlled by the labor of cats. Many humans liked the species *Felix cattus domestica* and were glad of a pragmatic excuse to keep cats as companion animals on farms. Rats were extinct all over the Earth. Nobody minded.

Lizzy finished her morning's chores by milking the sixth cow, Elsie, her favorite. Then she and Suzie — accompanied by two Jack Russell terriers and a golden retriever — walked back to the Earthship® residence together, wheeling their large, full, multigallon milk container with Lizzy's special friend, the calico cat named Cleo, riding smugly on the flat cover.

They would store the milk in *Stasis* for the needs of their communards and people on the farms around them who did not keep cows or goats. Pasteurization was unnecessary, as disease organisms — such as those causing typhoid fever, tuberculosis, salmonella, small pox, etc — once common in cattle — had long ago been deliberately eliminated from the Earth and were totally extinct.

Besides naturally holding more nutrients than pasteurized milk, *raw cows' milk* — according to many people in the past who had tried both — *tasted better.*

Breakfast — most of it harvested from food plants grown inside the Earthship® itself — was a choice of hash brown potatoes, scrambled eggs, stuffed grape leaves, pickled hibiscus petals, buttered toast, whole red grapes, banana and melon slices, and coffee, with cups of milk, iced tea, or freshly squeezed orange juice at the large dining table in Yellowood-Earthship®'s sunlit kitchen / GatherRoom. The food was 'help yourself', because the cooks refused to serve when they could already be eating their own breakfasts.

After a hasty shower, Lizzy, bootless and barefoot, sat down with her plate of food and stretched her long legs beneath the dining table, surveying her fellow communards — in varying shades of melanin skin colours — as they broke their overnight fasts that spring morning. They were a typical group of thirty-seventh-century humans living in that passive-solar Earthship®, and Lizzy was fond of them all, her shipmates in farming.

▼

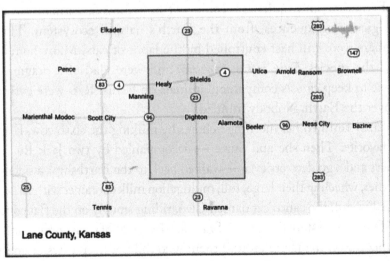

map of Lane County

Sitting side by side, both typically brown-skinned, were Bob Beiler, his short beard curly with grey, and Dillon Ness, portly and clean shaven. They were middle-aged lovers / partners, both wearing dark trousers and bright teeshirts, quiet and competent farmers.

Bob, 61, was an animal expert (as well as being *very* good with people), and Dillon, five months older, was a quiet farming-engineer who specialized in water recycling and reclamation. Unlike his partner, Dillon was not a people-person. He was more comfortable working with inanimate things, like the Earthship®'s water-use and filtering system. Dillon found humans much harder to effectively utilize. He preferred *things* he could grasp in his hands and easily manipulate. Both he and Bob were *high* graduates of Ness Village Agricultural University, several miles along K-96 to the west, in Ness County, the most prestigious agricultural-school in that general area of the Great Plains. In addition, Dillon had a second *high* degree from Atwood Village Engineering College further north in Rawlins County. Both men had been with Yellowood Farm for nearly four decades, over three decades as committed partners, and were the senior residents.

Mopping up her plate with a piece of toast was young Bekky Shields, 23, the Farm's food-coordinator, wearing green trousers and an '*island shirt*' in a pattern of bright colors: orange, red, yellow, deep-pink, purple flowers with green leaves, on a dark indigo field. Unusually pallid — her colourless skin, pale blonde hair, and blue eyes containing only a bare minimum of melanin — she tended the interior gardens, rather than work much outside, since she was susceptible to serious sunburn, having almost no ability to tan. New to Yellowood, having fallen in love with the farm at the end of her YouthTrip, she was the new eggmother of a baby boy — Hussein — who had just recently come to Yellowood Farm from the Dighton Village BirthHouse, where he had been gene-screened before conception and incubated in a replicant-womb as a fetus. His seedfather was George W.C. Healy, a lean, muscular, 25-years-young farming engineer, a *high* graduate of Atwood Village Engineering College, with mahogany coloured skin and kinky red hair. He had volunteered his sperm, stayed for the birth, and had then admitted he wanted to partner with Bekky in raising the boy (although the child would in reality be raised by all the communards as a community).

Undisturbed by the bustle of the farmers at breakfast, the tan-coloured baby with dark, curly Titian hair slept in a crib between his mother and father, his genetic-parents who also meant to be his Primary Parents.

Currently sitting together at the other end of the table from Lizzy, were Aisha McHenry and D'mitri Dauphin, bronze-skinned and identically attired in shorts and teeshirts, her neighbors who shared the toilet-room she used. They were young lovers in their early thirties, whose typical *'mixed race'* genetic material was, at their request, being screened for an optimum compatible match by techs at the BirthHouse in Dighton Village. They were soil and vegetable specialists respectively, tired of deep-snow winters, who had immigrated as a couple from an area much further north formerly known as Manitoba. The Yellowood communards were looking forward to another baby within the year.

Besides George-&-Bekky's Titian-haired offspring and the Dighton *'twins'*, Yellowood Farm had three other children, youngsters: two girls and a boy.

In addition, Yellowood housed a retired farmer, sepia-coloured, lean, nappy-haired Jameka Lunawanna, an elder 113 years old, retired as the farm senior. She had the prominent brow-ridges of her mostly Aborigine ancestors. An 'immigrant' from Tasmania — who had, on her YouthTrip, fallen in love with a Yellowood farmer and the flat *flat* landscape of the Great Plains, with its big, star-filled night sky, not dissimilar to the broad sky of the Australian Outback — she had spent all her adulthood at Yellowood Farm and now preferred to spend her last years relaxing, exercising the farm's telescope, and taking long walks, retired where she had spent her life. She was still sleeping in the same bedroom she had happily occupied for over ninety years with her partner now deceased.

So she wouldn't feel completely useless as a worker — which no human on Earth wanted to feel — Jameka occasionally helped Bekky the food-cord with food preparation, or played educational games with the little children. Many evenings (wearing special watch goggles), she viewed documentaries and Earth histories in the round on the 3D stage, or she kept her imagination active by reading a book from one of the many bookcases scattered throughout the Yellowood Earthship®, in the GatherRoom or in the various bedrooms of her shipmates.

There were no '*Old Age Homes*' on Earth. Elders were never forced out of the living situations they had known all their lives. Local health activists traveled from farm to farm, checking on all the elders in each county, rather than the retirees having to travel to see a healer, even in emergencies.

Older teenager Suzie Dighton, 19 — dressed for the day in cotton shorts and a blank, lime-green T-shirt, her black, kinky hair now 'civilized' into a neat cap — filled a plate with her food choices and sat down next to her pale-skinned 'twin', Manda Dighton. (The great difference in the skin colour of the 'twins' was not something people consciously noticed.) Manda — like her 'twin' and Lizzy — was a morning-person, and had gotten up at first bells to help Bekky prepare breakfast. She greeted Suzie's arrival with a warm, happy smile.

Suzie and Manda had been best friends at Yellowood Farm from babyhood, both decanted on the same day from replicant-wombs in the Dighton BirthHouse. They were not genetically related at all, but being the same exact age, they had been jokingly called '*twins*' all their lives.

Other shipmates of Yellowood's Earthship® completed the list of adult communards currently working the farm. First of all, sitting next to Lizzy, was stocky, small-breasted Torrin Beeler, 55 years old, a vegetable generalist, one of the large minority of humans whose gene-parents — with the help of techs at the BirthHouse where zee was born — had deliberately created hir intersexed as an hermaphrodite, adding to the variety of human genders. Torrin had always been happy about hir gene-parents' decision. Zee had had many lovers in hir life, both male and female. Many at first had just been curious about hermaphroditism, and then — since human beings generally tend to be bisexual — they had continued on with Torrin because zee was such a pleasant and enthusiastic lover. Nevertheless, zee had not yet found a permanent long-term partner and was happily open to whomever might come into hir life.

There was also Marsha Brownell, 35, a soil specialist, eggmother of two of the youngsters — Anelia and Edgardo — who had been seedfathered by Sheldon Rozel, 43, a horse whisperer and animal specialist. Also Ora Dighton, 32, un-partnered, often voluntarily solitary, apparently disinterested in sex, a vegetable-seed archivist and an engineer [like Dillon Ness, a *high* graduate of Atwood Village Engineering College]; and Jill Utica, 57, a general animal expert. Like Torrin, Jill was currently un-partnered, mother of a pre-teen girl, Bozena—whom she had bred with the Dighton BirthHouse Legacy-Sperm-bank.

All the Yellowood communards were wearing canvas shorts or trousers, and the common, ubiquitous, solid-color T-shirts.

"Oh Jill," Bekky said, "Nan the Vet called earlier. She's coming over later today to see bout Vilka's mastitis."

"Could see Vilka was stressed when milking her this morning," Suzie added. "Threw the milk in the compost bin. Lizzy had me isolate her in her stall and we got her calf to suckle from Bessie."

"Why'd this happen, eh?" D'mitri asked. "Don't yall animal specialists know how to prevent or cure such a minor disease in cows?"

"Mastitis is painful, so Vilka doesn't consider it a minor disease," Suzie said, frowning. Manda frowned too; she often copied her twin, consciously adding to the aura of their *'twin'* hood.

"And women in general don't," Bekky said, shuddering. George turned to her, looking concerned.

"D'mitri," Bob said. (He often stepped-in to prevent disagreements from escalating to real conflict.) "Been so many years since we had the problem, folks here at Yellowood don't know much bout it. Best to consult an expert. We're lucky to have such a competent and caring Vet here in Lane County."

"Aye," Jill said, grinning happily.

"Bekky," Dillon said, "if you're having a problem, tell us. Get you checked by our healer in Dighton."

"No," Bekky said. "I'm fine. Being a nursing mother, can just sympathize with Vilka."

"Glad t'hear you're okay," George leaned over the crib and hugged Bekky.

▼

All the communards were going to spend their morning in the outdoor garden harvesting early lettuce and such, thinning the beds, except for Lizzy, who had a rare scheduled holiday and had decided to insist on it. She wanted to go into the village, at the Dighton Library, to see a widely advertised, comprehensive, interactive, traveling hologram-and-video display of farmhouse choices all around the world. Although Earthships® were the most common type of residence, other architectural styles were used in other parts of the world. Lizzy was interested in seeing some geodesic-dome-shelters and other kinds of farmhouses.

Along with her skill as an animal expert, Lizzy also had an interest in anthropology and in architecture. Besides taking pride in her profession as a farmer — like 89% of the humans on Earth — and participating in all the work, preparation, rituals, and festivals of the agricultural year, she also intended, like most farmers, to keep up her intellectual interests. A life of research or teaching had not appealed to her. She believed — as did many people — *real work with one's hands was the most satisfying way to live*, a life of quiet, fulfilling routine, with independent study as a hobby or a second profession on the side.

▼

Before she left for her personal excursion, Lizzy went back with Suzie Dighton to the cool milk-processing room off the kitchen to finish their morning's chores: pour milk into *stay*glass bottles — glass made as unbreakable as steel by scientific advances six centuries earlier — and divide the bottles of milk between those intended for their communards to drink or process into cheese or butter, and those which would be delivered to other nearby farms within the week. They stored the extra milk in a *Stasis* cupboard.

▼

Lizzy left the residence by the west exterior door of the greenhouse corridor, taking steps up from the sunset porch and over the roof of the Earthship® where rainwater was collected and guttered into cisterns to provide water for the Earthship® to reclaim, cycle, filter, and recycle for drinking and cooking. The drinking water was used for washing humans and dishes; then water full of organic soap was used for automatic irrigation of the interior gardens; then '*graywater*' out of the interior gardens primed the toilets; and finally '*blackwater*' out of the flushed toilets was used as fertilizer for the trees, flowers, and other non-edible groundcover on the berm and on the north side of the Earthship®. (Dillon Ness oversaw and occasionally adjusted the entire water recycling system. He was well-known in the tri-county area for his advanced special talents. As a community service, Yellowood Farm was proud to lend Dillon's time, on those rare occasions when it was necessary, to other farms in Lane, Scott, or Ness Counties.)

Lizzy went to the farm's "front porch," a raised, wood floored, open-sided, oblong hut sitting against the stone wall of the earth berm—the *thermal wrap* of soil covering the northern side of Yellowood Earthship® and its cisterns. She sat on the "porch" swing to wait for the solar-powered minibus she had requested to pick her up. She could have ridden a horse, but did not want to be responsible for its care in the village while she was concentrating on her studies at the library. Better for the animal to stay home with the other horses and frolic in its own field.

She checked her personal, private eTablet to confirm the information she remembered about the exhibit. The *sci-fi* dream of turning human beings into semi-cyborgs by adding communication technology *inside* the body had long before been dashed by the unfortunate fact that direct electrical current so close to the human brain is very damaging. Technology had to remain outside the body, never close to neural tissue.

▼

Lizzy listened to the exquisite whispering of the quaking aspen trees (*Populus tremuloides*) long rooted in the underground blackwater grow-cell on and behind the berm covering Yellowood's Earthship®. The bright-yellow autumn color of the trees' leaves had long-ago inspired the farm's name.

Lazily rocking on the 'porch' swing, Lizzy gazed across the old two lane K-96 highway at Rosebud Farm's Earthship® residence—part of the local flotilla of solar-powered homes. It was an almost duplicate of Yellowood's Earthship®. She could see the sloped windows on the many-yards-long greenhouse corridor on the south side of the residence facing her. There was the usual long strip of solar panels above the windows, where they received full, direct sunlight for most of the day. Three windmills also contributed to the electricity Rosebud's Earthship® provided and stored for its inhabitants. Skylight dormers on the front edge of the roof helped to regulate heat and cooling in the summer.

Rosebud Farm extended northward for 130 acres in ' back' of the residence, growing wheat, oats, rye, etc for the county bread bakery in Dighton Village — as did several other farms in the area — to supply the populace of Lane County with their need for bread. Yellowood and other farms nearby shared some of the grain to feed their animals.

Rosebud's 'front yard' was an extensive rose garden where the communards of the Farm experimented with different strains and colors of roses, all fertilized with underground blackwater grow-cells.

Lizzy knew, like her own residence, Rosebud Earthship® held several bedrooms with a kitchen / GatherRoom area midway between. As well as the long greenhouse corridor in front filled to bursting with edible plants year round.

The solar-powered electric minibus came and stopped at Lizzy's 'porch'. She got on, greeted the driver—a young stranger new to the area—and seated herself in front where she had a wide view of the countryside going by. On a weekday — that early in the morning, before the area's teens would ride to their long afternoon of school in Dighton — the bus was nearly empty. Some of the seats held cartons of produce needed in the Village.

She enjoyed observing the local fleet of Earthships® — sometimes 200 yards apart — along old K-96. Each one was the thick-walled, passive-solar residence for a communal farm. All her life Lizzy had known that was how planet Earth was organized, as farms fifteen to twenty adults and their children could manage with minimal machinery. She had been taught in her teen history classes that farms carpeted the planet Earth everywhere except protected wilderness areas, the greenbelts, and the villages which housed communal facilities like BirthHouses, libraries, factories, and universities.

All of Earth's children grew up on farms. Everybody had a chance to live and work close to the Earth. The semi-wild greenbelts were available to everyone for renewal of the Spirit. Wild animals and plants had a compatible environment and were saved from extinction and human interference in the inviolate wilderness areas. Communally-shared food supplies were largely fresh and local. Every human and every companion-animal on Earth always had enough to eat.

The *peasant* population of Earth had no need for cities, which were in all cases highly radioactive rubble, and would be thus for billions of years. Only wilderness and rural areas, small villages and their physically isolated populations had survived the Final (Nuclear) War more than fifteen centuries before.

After the War, the Plutocratic Elites and their most useful servants had fled Earth for the possibility of less damaged planets elsewhere in the galaxy. Those left behind on Earth had cooperated across the globe to save themselves and salvage their few remaining resources. Their descendents, distant in time, still farmed the Earth in unconditional Solidarity, sharing food and everything else — as Poor people had always done, to survive — and they had built no more cities.

On the solar bus, Lizzy contentedly watched her part of Peasant-Earth go by. The Earthships® and their covering berms on the north side of K-96 were raised up on artificial hills. So the south-facing windows of their greenhouses would be above the dark shadow generated by the low winter sun shining behind the Earthships® close to them across K-96 to the south.

2
▼
THE INVADERS

The Starship was a cylinder 23 miles long, 12 miles in diameter, spinning on its long axis.

Inward from the 10 foot thick titanium wrap-around outer skin was 880 feet of solid lead and a half mile of H_2O-ice. Then the quarter-mile-wide cryo-chambers area with facilities for 400,000 clone soldiers frozen for the journey between the stars so they would be young and in peak physical condition when they arrived where they were needed for the Invasion.

Inward from cryo was a nearly quarter-mile-wide, wrap-around area of support systems for the operation of the starship, and in the lumen of the tube, on its inner surface, was the potential living space and the 'land' where food and other plants could be grown. Most of the 'land' was potentially for the raising of beef, because *real men need red meat.* The lumen of the tube was over 10 miles in diameter, large enough for clouds and a weather system, making almost 660 square miles of 'outdoor' living space on its inner surface, *the* 'land' of the Starship.

It had been designed as a generation ship, in case not enough soldiers survived the cryo process and the remaining remnant had to return home to Planet Faraday unfrozen over several generations, hopefully— even if the Invasion failed—with some of what they had come for.

The lumen of the Starship was illuminated by the twenty-mile long sun-tube, nano-built of artificial diamond-crystal molecules. The land was being used for military exercises to retrain Tom, Bill, and the other cryo-soldiers for the inevitable ground war in the Invasion to come.

In practice, the soldiers easily conquered the robots who were programmed to act like *the damned cowardly 'peacenik' descendents of the Losers,* inevitably the only humans still left on Earth. . . .

▼

After the exercises, Tom and Bill returned to the room they shared with two other men, all of them privates. The two friends had the place to themselves that afternoon.

"Damnit," Tom growled. "I'm sick of this shit." He was sitting on his bed which he had been forced to make-up *neatly* every day, something he had never done as a civilian living by himself.

"Hopefully," Bill said, "the officers are right, and the Invasion will win fast. Then they'll freeze us again and we'll return to our lives on Faraday."

"I'm not looking forward to killing real people, instead of robots," Tom said gloomily. "It makes me sick to think of it."

"I know. Me too," Bill said. "This expedition was ruined as soon as the military took it over."

"I think we're in trouble if we steal women from the Earthers rather than inviting them to voluntarily return to Faraday with us," Tom said. "Children born from the bodies of slaves can hardly be superior to those from artificial uteri."

"Actually," Bill said, "sadly, the actual emotional state of the women who gave birth to babies for all of Earth's history had little or no effect on the babies themselves. And Faraday needs to return to the old-fashioned genetic re-combining of sexual reproduction."

"Aren't women people?" Tom moaned.

"I don't know," Bill answered. "Maybe."

▼

Once all the military-exercises were over, the men were — as usual for sexual recreation — divided between the majority — bisexuals who could function as homosexuals — and the minority who were recalcitrant heterosexuals, not bisexual (nor homosexual) enough to perform sexually with the other men.

Tom Worthington and Bill McCarthy were best friends from University, and buddies in academic (and then military) matters, but never in sex. At the sound of the sex-recreation call, Bill waved and parted from Tom, walking away beside their Squad's Sergeant — Keith Richardson, a career soldier — who had a possessive arm across Bill's shoulders.

Tom watched with envy, wishing for the umteenth time he was not so stubbornly heterosexual and that his sex-rec time could be more genuinely friendly, with real people, not a manufactured occasion with videos and robot vaginas.

He went with the other het-men, each individual man naked and tense with sexual need, all of them ignoring each other. Their sex facility was a simulated 'night club' with a dance floor crowded with robot women gyrating to old-fashioned thud-thudding music meant to encourage the men's sexual desires. The walls displayed old, refurbished videos of real women which had been made in the night clubs of the cities of Earth — or made in that fabled magic place called Hollywood — long before the Final Nuclear War and the Star Exodus.

While other men danced with the robots, Tom (as well as a few other het-men) preferred to stand in front of one of the screens playing the old videos of real women. They were all so achingly beautiful with their long smooth legs, teetering on the spike-heeled shoes only women could wear — throwing their body's weight onto their toes, so deliciously kitten-like — emphasizing their long, long legs in their skirts, their *very* short skirts — women's sexy clothing never worn by men — their womanly legs going up, up, *up* into their skirts, enticing thoughts of the warm wet vaginas God had made especially for the use and pleasure of men. Women's bodies so soft and smooth and hairless, with their round, soft breasts bursting from the tops of their dresses. . . .

Finding himself hard enough, Tom turned from the video wall to stride onto the dance floor, find a robot dancing alone, (molded and dressed to look 'exactly' like the real women in the videos), that no other man wanted at that moment. He gripped its — no! *her, her,* always think *her!* — arm, and led *her* to one of the small bedroom alcoves curtained

off the main room. He climbed onto the alcove's bed to enter the robot
— woman, *woman!* — and satisfy himself.

Since the time he was a pubescent hetero-male, Tom had learned
not to look into the robot '*woman's*' eyes. The first time he had, joyful
with his first sexual experience, he had seen how greatly lacking in self
awareness the robot was. Its eyes were horribly empty. They were *dead*
eyes, devoid of humanity, or even of Life. Tom had been nauseous. He
had not been able to bear it. He wanted the 'woman' with whom he was
having sex to be a person, a self-aware *person*, and as joyful as he was to
be sharing sexual pleasure.

So since that time many years ago when he was very young, Tom
had always closed his eyes and imagined he was in coitus with a real
woman like those in the videos on the 'night club' walls. He no longer
expected joy in his sexual relations with robot '*women*'. Simply relief
of tension. Never release for his hungry heart. He wished, yet again,
it was possible for him to enjoy sex with his friend Bill, someone he
loved.

As always, as he experienced his barely-satisfying orgasm, Tom
hated his Faradayan ancestors who had succumbed to the new planet's
indigenous virus — or prion, *whatever* it was — which had somehow
aggravated their species inherent xenophobia (fear of strangers): First
they had slaughtered the few humans who were horribly different
because of their darker skin colour. And then they had murdered all
humans without a penis who were thus heinously maimed and different
from genuine humans who were male and white.

Their planet's reproductive crisis therefore had been aggravated
through the inevitable *replicative fading* over time of their cloning
process. The ability to cryo-freeze clone zygotes several generations
ahead helped only the oldest son in each 'family', who was privileged,
by Faradayan law, to unfreeze and develop each generation, in an
artificial uterus, one clone-zygote of their original progenitor. All
other sons had to clone themselves, so after very few generations,
replicative fading had set in, often producing damaged, inferior
children.

And beside the reproductive problems, Tom personally hated his ancestors for the sexual misery of all men on Faraday who were not homosexual or bisexual, but irredeemably heterosexual.

Oh! for a real woman! Tom had often prayed.

3

▼

PEASANT-EARTH

The inside of her head glowing with the intellectual pleasure of *learning* — that is, making new neurological connections in her brain — Lizzy Alamota left the Dighton Library's excellent walk-through, interactive exhibit of holograms and videos of global farmhouse architecture and strolled to the corner of Long (old K-96) and Main Streets at the center of Dighton Village. As she crossed the street, a low, round, street-cleaner-robot bumped her ankle. She was uninjured. Her foot against its rubber bumper — without conscious regard — Lizzy adjusted its trajectory.

She entered the Village Cafeteria, an Earthship® open for supper, designed to serve food in-house and take-out to the Dighton public and visitors. The south facing, sloped windows were familiar, and the wide greenhouse corridor jungle-like with edible plants. The interior had two large, near-capacity dining areas in use to the east and west, separated on either side of the large, central kitchen by the serving tables. There she got herself an 'eat-in' helping of cricket casserole, a delicious blend of baked crickets — sans legs, head, antennae, ovipositors, and wings — with onions, hot spices, and diced root vegetables. It was a crunchy, 'exotic,' protein dish, a favorite of hers not often available at Yellowood Farm.

Insects, while not cows, goats, or chickens, are still in the Animal Kingdom, and thus not a '*kosher*' part of a vegetarian diet. However, crickets, like grasshoppers and locusts, are *kosher* in the Biblical sense, having '*their knees above their heads*' — (Leviticus: 11:21) — of the scientific Order *Orthoptera* (insects whose hind legs are enlarged for jumping).

After her 'exotic' supper, Lizzy crossed Main Street to the thick walled, cob-built Dighton BirthHouse, entirely electric and climate controlled, powered by photovoltaics and five small windmills on its wide roof. Whenever she was in Dighton, she always liked to check on the ovary she had stored in Stasis (Entropy-Stopped) — as did most girls — when she was thirteen. At the same time, the fallopian tube connecting her other ovary to her uterus had been valved off, so — while enjoying normal hormone levels — she didn't have to worry about unwanted pregnancy and could behave like a sexually-free person.

▼

"Hi. I'm Lizzy Alamota. I'd like to visit my ovary," Lizzy said to the handsome copper-coloured young man at the reception desk in the BirthHouse. He sported a thin black mustache and wore a pink T-shirt saying: 'Dighton BirthHouse' curved above the BirthHouses' circled logo, a human hand tenderly cupping a healthy 11-week-old fetus.

"I'm Ben Ransom. We'll go right back to the stasis-vault," he said. "Kerrin, could you fill in here for me? Thanks. Come on now, Lizzy."

In the dim, reddish-lit vaults, Ben stood discretely aside, in case the depositor might need assistance.

Lizzy plugged her personal eTabb and fingerprints into the search unit on the exam table. She didn't have to wait long until her ovary was auto-delivered to her.

It looked like any other ovary, about four centimeters at its greatest length. Checking it several times a year was customary, to insure both that it remained viable and that it was not lost in the system. First of all, she checked the flat bottom of the *stay*glass container to make sure the permanent identifying barcode was not scratched or otherwise permuted. She wiped off the signature plate on the base and re-signed and re-dated it. The seal was unbroken, so her ovary had not been removed from its transparent stasis-jar since she had seen it last and had thumb-printed the seal. Satisfied with the condition and safety of her ovary, she sent it right back to the BirthHouse's extensive below-ground stasis-vault. Then she joined Ben for the walk back to the BirthHouse lobby.

"Thanks Ben. It's great of you folks to always let us check on our ovaries," Lizzy said.

"Such precautions are really not necessary," he said, "since BirthHouses have always had great procedures for keeping genetic materials safe."

"Yall have a proud, and necessary, profession, Ben. But the rest of us got to keep yall on your toes."

"Well, you know all BirthHouse Workers promise, under hypnosis, while being holo-filmed, to respect the Rights of every single person— woman, man, trans, or herm—who deposits their genetic material with us in the BirthHouses. Interference with the absolute freedom of any person's reproductive-rights is one of those filthy customs from the Elite Ages we totally reject."

"Aye," Lizzy said, taking his arm companionably. "Is why everybody has such respect for your profession, even though yall — like everyone — were raised to be farmers, then left it."

"We think of ourselves as farmers of the future human race," he said, grinning at her and patting her hand on his arm. "And well, even though most of us live in the village, our Earthships® have large gardens." We're farmers still."

"Ah, so you think of yourselves as the greatest farmers of all? Hmm?"

"The BirthHouses couldn't do their job if everyone didn't trust us."

"Well, we do."

"And that's good," he said. "Because for fifteen centuries, since all the various technologies of genetic selection and replicant-womb reproduction were perfected, that Trust has never been broken, anywhere in the world. . . .

"We Workers in the BirthHouses," he continued, "feel responsible both for facilitating every person's reproductive-freedom, and also for monitoring the population of the Earth so it doesn't increase as fast as it did before the Final War. Did they teach you in teen school how in 2561, four centuries after the Final War, the Global Free-Association-of-BirthHouse-Workers had to tell the People of Earth that the world population was rising again, much too quickly? And if all of us didn't commit to having only two children per breeding pair, we were soon going to overwhelm our planetary resources? Fortunately, we had that new, egalitarian, ConsensusCentral programming to help us, so we could decide all-together what to do bout the crisis."

"Uh, aye. I guess I remember something like that from history class."

"BirthHouse Workers study that crisis as part of our training. We hoped the problem could be solved by all of us behaving voluntarily. That everyone would essentially breed to replace themselves with a child of usually the same gender. So we wouldn't have to abandon our Anarkhy, a least in the BirthHouses, and begin somehow compelling people to cooperate for the good of the planet and our inheritors. Most of us hoped that the Trust would never be broken, and that everyone's Reproductive Freedom would forever remain unmolested by any kind of Authority."

"That's when the idea of the Legacy-Egg-banks and the Legacy-Sperm-banks started, wasn't it?"

"Aye! If a person is so egotistical they think they should have more descendents than other people, they can will their genetic material after their death for the future use of anyone who might want it to avoid partnering with a live person for reproduction, or who might want to add variety to their farm's children. Or who want to acquire for their children, and for the future, those special, what-were-once-rare-traits like perfect pitch, violet-colored eyes, tetrachromatism (ability to see millions of different shades of colors), or even immunity to the common-cold, a mild, multi-virus disease not so common any more."

"Well," said Lizzy, "here we are. The lobby."

"Um, maybe you could come back sometime and we could have lunch?"

"Great," she said. "I live at Yellowood Farm. Call me. Our food-cord is a good cook."

"Okay."

▼

After leaving the BirthHouse, Lizzy went to the 3D Printing-Service Facility known in Dighton Village as 4D Printing. She had promised Dillon Ness she would get him a part he needed for Yellowood's water-reclamation system.

The shop's entrance bell dinged to announce her. "Hi," she said. "Lizzy Alamota, Yellowood Farm. Dillon Ness called you?" She consulted her eTabb. "We need a C-623A valve printed. Have the pattern on file?"

The worker who greeted her was a young man about the same tall height as she was, with jet black skin colour and black, short cut, neat, kinky hair. His handsome, smooth-skinned, muscular arms were exposed by his red sleeveless muscle-shirt. Lizzy thought he was very attractive. "Ty Galena," he said. "Nice to meet you. Have the specs for your valve on file. Print a lot of 'mm. Take a few minutes."

Lizzy sat down on a luxuriously padded bench to wait. "Seems to me that particular part wears out a lot. Wish someone would redesign it," she said.

Ty turned from typing the requisite program into the hot metals 3D printer and leaned comfortably on the counter, smiling at Lizzy. His black eyes flashed. "Think too many people opt for a Farmer's Life, stead more sedentary jobs improving our technology," he said.

"Can you blame umm?"

"No. Only staff this shop part time. Really a farmer. Live at TreeFruit Farm, three miles south of Dighton. Have the tallest Earthship® in North America," he said proudly.

"Aye. Yall's farm's Earthships® are part of the World Exhibition at the Library I just saw."

"Oh, that's great! Uh, bout the problem . . ." (He obviously had no interest in exhibitions of Earthships® other than his own.) "*Uh* . . . bout the valve . . . we were talking . . ?"

"Well, being a farmer *is* the best," Lizzy said. Like most farmers, she was arrogant about the value of her chosen profession. "Think we've got to figure how to make other professions —specially scientist, research engineer, or experimentalist—as attractive as farming."

"Half-Decade Continental-Meet is coming up next year, in Lindsborg Village, McPherson County," Ty said. "Could jointly reserve a chance to make a proposal uh . . . bout the problem and convince the Meeting to convene a WorkingCommittee."

"Not a bad idea."

"Can we get together over the next year and work out the details of our proposal?" he asked.

Ah! Thought Lizzy. *He's interested. Hope he's single. Can't do the polyamorous thing. Course, people can do what they like. Just not with me. . . .* "Good idea," she said. "Next week sometime?"

"Wednesday, 6PM. That's my day here at 4D. Closer for me four miles to Yellowood by bus than you going over five miles on meandering dirt roads through the greenbelts to TreeFruit on horseback after I take a bus ride three miles home." The printer beeped. "Oh! Here's your part finished. It's cooled."

"Thanks. See you next week."

▼

The minibus dropped Lizzy off on the north side of K-96, near Rosebud Farm. She crossed the road and took a flagstone path past the eastern berm of Yellowood's Earthship® to the sunrise patio and the eastern entrance of the residence's greenhouse corridor.

She walked down the sunny corridor with prolific greenery brushing her left shoulder, and halfway down, at the first banana plant, turned right and went into the GatherRoom of the Earthship®.

Nan Diller, DVM—a Lane County Veterinarian—had stayed for supper after attending the cow Vilka. The Vet, 48 years old, dressed in green T-shirt and trousers, was of short stature, not stocky but athletic, with short dark blonde hair, pale skin, violet eyes, and strong square hands with short nails. She had a high degree in Veterinary Science from Ness University.

Her horse was comfortably stabled in the Farm's thick-walled cob-barn and she was seated on the 3D stage in the GatherRoom's corner, wearing watch goggles, with a large tabby tomcat on her lap, viewing a 3D documentary—about undersea life—with retired senior Jameka Lunawanna, as well as Jill Utica, Jill's daughter Bozena (one of Yellowood's pre-teen girls), the '*twins*' Suzie and Manda, and partners Bob-&-Dillon. Goggled with headphones for '*experiencing*' the 3D, they all felt as though they were under the ocean, magically able to breathe, surrounded by marine creatures, easily hearing the moderator's commentary. To anyone ungoggled, the holograms flickered ghost-like in the air above the 3D stage. The Farm's dogs, phoxes, and cats, who couldn't wear goggles, ignored the insubstantial 'ghosts'. A JackRussel terrier— named 'Jack' by the children—slept on the floor of the '*ocean*', ignored by the humans and the holograms.

Torrin Beeler was taking dishes out of the washer and putting them away. George-&-Bekky were sitting at the kitchen prep table talking quietly with Torrin while Bekky nursed Hussein.

Waiting his turn at bottle-nursing using '*imported*' goat's milk, (George had declined the hormone treatments which would have rendered him capable of nursing his son with his own body, and would have temporarily interfered with his sexual functioning), George watched Bekky and their baby, his grin as wide as his face.

"Hey," Lizzy greeted the room at large and waved off an offer of seated space on the 3D stage. She sat down at the cleared dining table to view the notes she had made on her eTabb—at the Library's exhibition of farmhouse choices all around the world—and studied them. She took the water reclamation valve she had 3D-printed out of her pocket and waggled it in the air above her head while saying, "Dillon."

"Okay, thanks," he said.

Lizzy put the newly printed valve down on the table to await Dillon's pickup.

Later, Nan Diller stayed the night, obviously to Jill's delight. Nan was polyamorous, and had lovers all over Lane County.

Lizzy stayed up later than everyone else that night, hungrily going over and over her eTabb notes, craving to renew that first wonderful, fiery burst of intellectual pleasure inside her head, until she couldn't keep her eyes open any longer. . . .

4

▼

PEASANT-EARTH

A few days later, Bob-&-Dillon were awakened early in the morning when the Dighton '*twins*' crawled into the sheets with them. A German shepherd sleeping on the foot of their bed leaped off and left the room.

"Oh, Suzie, Manda . . . Oh . . . let me out . . . up . . . have to pee," Bob gasped.

"Me too . . . Girls, please . . . Will cuddle . . . just . . . let me up, up, oh!" Dillon added.

▼

Before the time the "twins" had turned three, both their pairs of young genetic-donors had coincidently ended their relationships, without rancor, and had left Yellowood Farm after the fall harvest, in four different directions, leaving behind their little, *barely-self-aware toddlers*.

In the centuries on Earth since the end of the Final War, because of the universal custom of taking pregnancy out of the bodies of individual women, babies and children had come to be thought of not as the "property" — and the exclusive responsibility — of their genetic donors but rather as belonging to — and the moral responsibility of — the village in which they had been "born." Thus the genetic material of young people from all over the Earth as they met and mingled during their YouthTrips was universally combined in the BirthHouses, creating a strong hybrid mix of the best traits of all of Earth's peoples. Thus the human species — the children of those rural people all over the Earth who had survived the Nuclear War — was strengthened with hybrid vigor; and everyone had a stable childhood nurtured on farms by people who chose to be PrimaryParents of healthy, *wanted* human children.

At that time, Bob-&-Dillon, more than twenty years into their committed relationship, had begun to talk together about going to the BirthHouse in Dighton and maybe breeding together with the complicated help of the BirthHouse techs. But then they decided — with the gratitude, in parting, of both the girls' genetic parent-pairs, because the two men had already begun to extensively share the care of Suzie and Manda — that instead they would accept Primary Responsibility for nurturing the 'abandoned' *'twin'* toddlers.

The *'twins'* had, throughout their childhoods, often crept, as children will do, into the bed of their Primary-Parents, for reassurance in the wake of a nightmare, ease of late night loneliness, or just for cuddling. Bob-&-Dillon had always been glad to comply.

▼

"Okay!" Both men came back from the toilets together and burst into their bedroom, wearing the unwrinkled sleeping shorts and teeshirts they had hastily donned. They climbed into bed with the girls — their 'babies' — and settled down to cuddling.

"Well," Bob said, gently cupping Suzie's crisp, kinky hair, "neither yall girls did this since yall were . . . twelve, wasn't it, Dil?"

"Aye, think twelve," Dillon answered, hugging Manda.

Suzie chuckled, "When we hit puberty, realized — both of us hetero — had to stop crawling into bed with naked men."

"Hadn't noticed before, we sleep raw?" Dillon asked, also chuckling.

"Nobody pays attention to that stuff til they hit puberty," Manda said.

"Stuff!" Bob hissed.

The men looked at each other.

"Guess yall're right," Dillon said.

"So, why the flattery of this occasion so early in the morning?" Bob asked.

"Today is our last day at the farm," Suzie said.

"We have to leave," Manda whispered, and cuddled closer to Dillon. "*Have* to leave?" Bob asked. "Don't yall girls want to leave on yall's YouthTrips?"

"Aye, want t'go see the rest of the world," Suzie said, "but we're, uh . . ."

"Scared," Manda said.

"The world is safe," Bob said. "Of course."

"Long as—without competent guides—you stay out dangerous places like, umm . .," Dillon added, "mountaintops, swamps, fast rivers, and . . . all wilderness conservation areas."

"Few survive an attack by a wild animal," Bob said.

"Will miss yall," Manda said.

"Everybody," Suzie added.

"And all will miss yall," Dillon said. "But we're not in stasis. Life is not stasis. You both have to grow up."

"And get old, eventually," Bob added. "Unfortunately, Dillon and I have already started getting old. Life is short, even at an average of 130 years."

"You ain't old," Manda said, wide eyed, grabbing Dillon's cheeks by the beginnings of his jowls.

"Might be, time you get back, if you ever return to visit," Bob said. "Remember, custom is at least three years away from the area where you grew up, preferably in a completely different biome. Least a different continent."

First-bells sounded throughout the Earthship®, intending to wake those communards whose chores started early.

"That's me," Suzie said. "Last day with Lizzy milking cows."

"Have to help with breakfast, my last day with Bekky," Manda added.

"We might as well help with breakfast too," Dillon said.

"No." Bob snapped. "I have something else in mind."

"Oh?" Dillon asked, grabbing the waistband of his shorts.

"Come on, Suzie. Time for us to leave," Manda said, grinning.

▼

The communards did the absolute minimum of chores that morning, and then ate lunch together before the gift-giving ceremony held in their GatherRoom to equip their beloved children for their YouthTrips.

"Usually don't have two children leaving at the same time," Bob said. "Equipping yall took some planning. These arrived at Rosebud Farm from the factory in Ness Village for us to secretly pick up only yesterday." He threw off a tarp.

"Bicycles!" both girls exclaimed. The gift of personal non-organic transportation (not horses) was traditional, but they hadn't seen or heard anything and were beginning to worry. . . .

The bicycles were identical, painted a deep yellow — with pale green and brown stripes — to remind them of Yellowood Farm.

In addition, Suzie and Manda each received a backpak; a new set of traveling clothes; new toothbrushes; extra underwear; and new hiking boots, hand crafted in modern, breathable, organic vat-leather to fit their feet exactly, as all footgear was in their global society. Long ago, the craft of shoe making — rescued from profit-taking mass production — had been, all over the world, entrusted to people who happily worked with their hands.

The girls were also presented with their first adult eTabbs. As Kids of the Farm they had up until then only used the farm's larger, old fashioned, not very portable, limited eTabbs. The girls began to get excited about their YouthTrips, and set about transferring their personal information from the Farm's child-eTablets to the new, private eTabbs they would use the rest of their lives.

▼

The communards started getting set up for the farewell party on their Lawn just off the sunset porch outside the western exit of Yellowood Earthship®'s greenhouse corridor. The Lawn was a half-acre completely level on a base of sandy loam soil planted with tightly-sheared creeping BentGrass, typically kept trimmed with a special hand mower to 3/16 of an inch.

Caring for the Lawn was one of the daily chores at Yellowood Farm, with constant vigilance against insect attack. The communards used a super-biotic spray made from organic dish-soap, glycerin, and various spices mixed with the essential oils of sundry other plants like citronella, witch hazel, and especially-imported cajuput oil. The bug spray was applied almost daily, early in the morning, so no one needed to be afraid at any time to dance barefoot, practice yoga, or do other exercises while naked on the Lawn.

The volunteer, neighborhood band set themselves up on the edge of Yellowood's sunset porch. The band included musicians and instruments from Grasshopper Farm (next door, 185 yards to the east), Pinklight Farm (219 yards to the west of Yellowood, where the Pinklight farmers grew coffee and several kinds of tropical vegetables and fruits year round, indoors under flickering pinklight), and Rosebud Farm (just across K-96). Tables for potluck food sat on the porch behind the band, up against the brick walling the berm.

▼

The farewell party, attended by friends and neighbors from as far away as Dighton Village, began after the Yellowood communards had supper. Included were many of the twins' schoolmates from Dighton teen-school, where the farm's older children had gone every afternoon and early evening after graduation from Dighton's first-school (ages 8 to 12, meeting mornings in the village before lunch).

Before they went to first-school, children younger than eight years old were taught on their home farms how to do simple arithmetic, as well as how to read and write in their local ethnic language and in *Esperanto*, the global language. As they all worked alongside the adults, they learned basic farm skills, like simple botany and animal care. As well, traveling teachers on a monthly basis visited each flotilla (neighboring group) of Earthships® in every county or province on Earth, to bring holographic, creative learning experiences of all sorts to eager groups of young farm children (and interested adults).

▼

Barefoot, Suzie and Manda joined their classmates, neighbors, and fellow communards in the dancing, moving to the band's music in the custom of their Age. All the dancers circulated through the crowd independently, as each of them chose, interacting with others spontaneously to form patterns — dancing in circles, couples, triads, quads, quints — coming together and separating, the designs briefly distinct, apparently complicated, familiar, and then dissipating. . . .

Everyone continued dancing as each individual felt inspired to do. The twins danced with bittersweet joy amid the community which had nurtured them from birth. As they moved around the lawn, people stopped and hugged and kissed them, their interactions making brief, tender knots in the shifting patterns of the larger dance.

The music shook everyone, deliciously rattling their innards, especially the **boom!** **boom!** of the African and Native American drums played fast and hard, filling everyone with joy and delight.

Lizzy Alamota cavorted with her usual flair, exalting in briefly being part of each pattern as it formed, happy to be moving to the music exactly as she pleased, swinging her hips, arms and legs in almost tai-chi movements, loving the feel of the lawn's fine grass beneath her bare feet. Her mind settled into an almost meditative state as she pranced about the lawn in solidarity with the other dancers, her farm-neighbors and beloved shipmates, celebrating her own freedom and that of Yellowood's children, Suzie and Manda.

Companion animals — dogs, cats, and red-furred, pointy-nosed phox — sat around the border of the lawn, watching the humans and their 'crazy' gyrations, playing with each other to exercise their excitement.

(Researchers in Siberia had long ago patiently bred from the wild fox the domesticated, cuddly, genetically-tamed-fox (*Volpes volpes domestica*), later nick-named the "phox.")

An hermaphrodite, Torrin Beeler of Yellowood Farm was a drummer in the community band. Hir movements with the heavy batons were much more flamboyant than hir calm gestures while putting dishes away in the Earthship®. Many of the dancers — stamping their feet, lifting their knees — followed hir popular, quick, staccato drumbeats: *drrumm,* **boom dumm,** *dum dumm,* **boom dum,** *drrumm,* **boom,** *drrumm . . .* The drums **boomed** in exultation.

Lizzy — not a bad drummer herself — ultimately came over to relieve Torrin: "Okay, Shipmate," she said, gently patting hir shoulder. "Let me drum awhile. Go exercise your own feet. Remember we're scheduled to do this all over again for Trayvon Dighton at Pinklight Farm in two days."

Torrin smiled at her, hir dark face shining with sweat.

All over the Earth, spring was the traditional time for YouthTrips and the bittersweet, euphoric celebration of farewell dances.

5

▼

THE INVADERS

Tom Worthington crouched beside his friend Bill in the crowded cavernous hold of the winged troop-transport jet shuttle. He was wearing a parachute over a personal jetpack and a fireproof flightsuit covered with zippered pouches. So clothed, he felt unpleasantly damp and sticky all over. He held an automatic weapon in his clammy hands. He had been 'checked out' on the weapon in basic training nearly 100 years before — which actually seemed like last week to him — but he wasn't sure he remembered anything about it. He was sick to his stomach, anticipating his first real experience of combat, with the horrifying prospect of having to actually kill other human beings. People who were unarmed.

Striding through the crowd of crouching soldiers, their Squad Sergeant reached Tom and Bill, roughly hustling them toward the hold's bay doors open to glaring sunlight and the bright blue. Compulsively clutching the edge of the opening, Tom experienced an eternity of sheer terror, turning his face away from the vertigo-inspiring emptiness . . . too brief . . . until Sergeant Richardson snapped a line from each of their parachutes to a ring on the bay opening, and shoved them out into the sky.

Tom screamed as he fell, hearing other men around him in the sky screaming also. There hadn't been time — in the hasty Basic Training they had received a hundred years before on planet Faraday — to train the draftees in parachute jumping.

Then Tom's parachute was jerked open by his line connected to the shuttle. It was a shock as the sudden change in rate of fall painfully seemed to rearrange all his bones. He fought to breathe. The sky was full of parachutes. He looked down and could see Kansas City, all concrete with dark rivers snaking through it, the image fuzzy for some reason. . . . Probably his fear-filled eyes.

Other squadrons of Faradayan soldiers, at the same time, all over Planet Earth, were in the same way invading other major cities: Sydney, New York, Vienna, Singapore, Rio de Janeiro, Paris, Reykjavik, Oslo, Copenhagen, and every other city the Invaders thought would hold a good population of pale-skinned women.

The fifteen hundred Faradayan soldiers involved in the assault on Kansas City, including privates Tom and Bill, had been assured the Invasion would be a surprise. The Earthers would not have time to mobilize and shoot down the parachuters dangling so helplessly in the air over their unprotected cities.

Just like the thousands of soldiers invading other cities, their mission was to descend on the metropolis and do as much damage as possible to the infrastructure. Then each soldier was to return, using his personal jetpack, to the winged shuttles with at least one — preferably more — kidnapped, young, apparently fertile, pale-skinned women as captives.

The men of Faraday had learned cloning was not a viable means of reproduction over many generations. They needed women for sexual reproduction, to create new genomes, not copied genomes, or they and their fine, capitalist, meritocratic, hierarchical civilization would rapidly go extinct. Already, good clones — exact copies — were often impossible to produce.

▼

There was a dome of sorts over the city. Looking down through his dangling feet, Tom watched it approach. Other men reached it before him, their boots striking sparks on the transparent surface. Some of the men fired their old-fashioned weapons at the dome, trying to break into the city. The steel bullets ricocheted, hitting some of the shooters, and others who hadn't shot.

Tom's feet grounded on the dome, throwing up sparks. The surface beneath his booted feet felt *fizzy*. How were they going to get into the city? Having seen what happened before he landed, Tom was not stupid enough to fire his weapon at the dome. He looked around for Bill. Other soldiers were still firing their guns at the surface underfoot. Tom saw Bill fall, hit by a ricochet, and frantically ran to him.

His Sergeant landed beside them, shouting to the men in his squad, "Cease fire! Cease fire, you lugs! Cease fire!" He immediately addressed the wound in Bill's side. "Medic!" he screamed.

▼

Keith Richardson, the Squad's Sergeant, concluded immediately that the Colonels were wrong: the Earthers were *not* *un*-protected. The cities had some sort of high tech hemispheric Shields which were impervious to gunfire. As a medic worked on fixing Bill, the Sergeant radioed his superiors through a small, radio transfer satellite off-planet in space at the stable Lagrange Point **L4** and thus to the starship hiding at **L2** 932,057 miles from Earth behind the Moon. At the speed of light [186,282+ *miles per second or* 300,000+ *kilometers/sec*], radio waves made the round trip through **L4** to **L2** and back in over nineteen seconds, making the conversation feel irritatingly disjointed and slow. Although they weren't actually under fire from the Earthers, the Sergeant was nevertheless vibrating in combat mode.

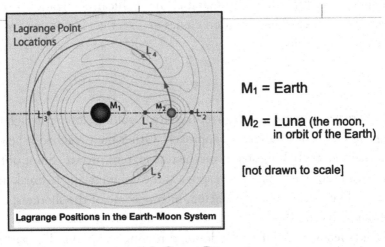

M_1 = Earth

M_2 = Luna (the moon, in orbit of the Earth)

[not drawn to scale]

Lagrange Positions in the Earth-Moon System

LaGrange Points

"Squad 14 calling Headquarters." There was the wait of over nineteen seconds while the radio photons made the trip through **L4** to **L2** and the Colonels' answer returned over the same distance.

"Headquarters; Colonel Billings here. Over," the Sergeant's radio squawked in his ear.

"Sir, we are at Kansas City. The Earthers have some sort of energy dome over our target. And I think . . . uh . . . the city may not actually be inhabited. Over."

The wait for an answer was annoying: "Other positions are reporting the same, Sergeant. Tell your other Squad Leaders. Transfer to the ground. When the tanks arrive, try their larger guns on the Shield. Over."

Master Sergeant Richardson conferenced by radio with the Sergeants of other squads. It was after sunset before those soldiers still living and not severely wounded — those remaining of the original fifteen-hundred-man Kansas City Invasion Force — were transferred to the ground on the east side of the apparently impregnable dome. All casualties were 'friendly fire,' inflicted by uselessly firing at the surface of the EnergyShield. The jet shuttle had landed and delivered the fast, low-slung, flexible mini tanks crowned by their big guns.

The Tanker soldiers used bright lights to check out their equipment, and the first tank available was set up facing the EnergyShield over Kansas City, at a distance thought safe from ricochets. Bright lights revealed a ruined, empty, suburban neighborhood burned out just inside the totally transparent wall of the EnergyShield.

"Fire!" Sergeant Richardson roared.

The EnergyShield remained impervious. Ricochets destroyed a group of invasion soldiers working under floodlights setting up sleeping tents for the squads off at a 30 degree angle from the line of fire. The Faradayans had not expected *any* casualties in their war with the '*loser-men*' of Earth.

Sergeant Richardson reported to the Colonels who agreed that, for practical purposes, the EnergyShield was indeed invulnerable. "What now, Sir?" Richardson asked, waiting without patience while the radio photons *crawled* through **L4** to the starship at **L2** and back.

"Don't forget, Sergeant, what this invasion is all about. You must procure women. That's what Faraday needs. What we — as the premier example of human civilization in all the Galaxy — need. So never mind destroying the infrastructure of the Losers' so called 'civilization'. That would only be icing on the cake. Just capture as many women — with pale skin, don't forget — as many women as you can. Kill the males and all the Darkies.

"After we leave Earth, with all the women we need to give us strong new sons, this filthy planet can go back to the cockroaches. Earth was useless garbage when we left it fifteen centuries ago, and it still is. The left-behind-losers have made it a shit-floored food factory, growing vegetables. Vegetables! Bet none of them ever eat steak, like real men. Their standard of living is so low — all of them ignorant peasants — they'll hardly notice when they're dead.

"Put 'um all out of their disgusting misery."

6

▼

PEASANT-EARTH

At Yellowood Farm, late morning after the day-before Farewell Party:
"Come see the news! Come on! Come on!" Edgardo Dighton called
out. He was a skinny, brown pre-teen wearing only ragged shorts in the
day's heat. "Invasion!!"

"What! Who?" Lizzy Alamota asked the excited youngster. She
was shirtless, wearing thin cotton shorts, sweat running down her
sides, currying a horse, working in the sunlit barnyard with Sheldon
Rozel.

"Us! Us! Earth!"

"Who's invading us?" she asked.

"Space! News says they come from space! Soldiers, soldiers!"
Edgardo cried. "Come see!"

"Sheldon, come on! To the Ship!" Lizzy put down her brushes and
rags and followed Edgardo as he ran back into the Earthship®.

▼

As Lizzy came into the cooler GatherRoom, she saw several of
Yellowood's communards grouped around the large 2D screen, watching
the shocking news as it was transmitted live from tiny robo-cams in
flight over the cities of Earth as the Invaders attacked.

"Ha!" Ora Dighton remarked. "EnergyShields are holding."

"Course they are," Dillon Ness said. "They've protected us from the Final War's alpha, beta, and gamma radiation from the ruined cities all these fifteen hundred years."

Marsha Brownell said, "But physical attack against the Shields is different from creeping radiation. . . ."

"The City-Shields were tested with weapons left over from the Final War when they were first put up," George W.C. Healy said. "They'll hold."

"Won't they be weaker with age?" Martha asked.

"No," Ora said. "Engineers in each region test each of our Farm-Shields every decade — don't yall remember? — if they haven't in that time been used against natural disasters — in our case, tornados — to be sure they'll continue to hold. And the strength of all our Shields are based on those decade-tests as well as the Shields' performance in disasters."

"Will have to rely on our FarmShields as soon as the Invaders abandon their useless attacks on the cities. They'll soon realize they're empty of people," Sheldon said quietly.

"Who are the Invaders, eh?" Aisha McHenry asked.

Just then — eerily as if in answer to her question — the robo-cams focused on several invaders struggling atop the EnergyShield over Singapore. ""They're humanoid!" Lizzy cried.

"Aliens from outer space would not be shaped anything like humans," brown-skinned Anelia Dighton said with all the conviction of a fifteen year old. The distinction between science fiction and scientific realism was fresh in her mind, since she was still in teen-school. "Have the Elites come back to make us slaves again?" she asked. She moved to hug her seedfather — Sheldon Rozel — while he put his arm around her protectively, and his other arm around her eggmother, his lover and partner, Marsha Brownell.

"Okay, come on Ora, George," Dillon said. "Let's talk to the other engineers at Rosebud Farm and prepare to set up our joint partnership FarmShield."

The soft, melodious trumpets of the farm's phone rang. George, nearby, answered it. "Hello. Yellowood Farm. George Washington Carver Healey speaking." His communards could hear the pride in his voice because he shared the name of that famous former slave, botanist, inventor, and environmentalist from the USA's post-slavery times who had created — among a myriad of other foods — peanut butter. "Sure. Aye. Will meet yall there."

"Rosebud?" Dillon asked.

"Aye."

"Let's go. I've got the tools," Ora said.

The three Yellowood engineers, accompanied by a German shepherd and a Labrador retriever, left the residence by the greenhouse corridor's east door, crossed the sunrise patio, and followed the flagstone path to the back of the Earthship® — to the 'front porch', where Lizzy had waited for the solar bus — beside K-96. The Rosebud engineers — accompanied by an Alaskan husky — were already there, having only to cross the street from their front yard. They had already unhooked the 'porch' swing and set it aside, and were removing the floorboards of the 'porch' to get at the Shield's controls.

It suddenly started to rain, a typical summer downfall. The roof of the 'porch' protected the exposed controls. The dogs barked and sniffed at the blinking lights. It was their job to protect the humans from anything unusual.

Dillon said, "Let's turn on the Shield, to make sure it's working, but then leave it off 'til we're sure we need it. We could use the rain. Our water reserves are lower than I like, since we face a siege."

"Us too," said one of the Rosebud engineers. She was a dark-brown middle-aged woman with prominent features — Dalla Dighton — wearing a red straw hat crowned with a real purple rose. She was shirtless and bare breasted in the heat, sporting a flowered full skirt.

George manipulated the controls. The Farm-Shield crackled and came on immediately. The rain suddenly ceased to fall on both Yellowood and Rosebud Farms, particularly the roofs of the Earthships®, which collected the rainwater. The dogs barked again.

"Okay," Ora said, after they had checked all the readings. "Need in place some robo-cams— we got any? — to watch for invading flyers or ground troops nearby." She was cuddling with the Labrador retriever named Max, her special friend.

"Have a few I picked up at the last Decade Continental Meeting," young Ryder LaCrosse from Rosebud said. He was well-muscled, dark skinned, shirtless, and barefoot in soft canvas shorts. "Somebody will have to monitor at all times."

"Have a few robo cams too," George said. "Can each monitor our own and raise the Farm-Shield the instant we think necessary."

"Aye. Better safe than sorry," Ryder said. "Will keep in touch."

"Should watch twenty-four hours a day," Dillon said. "No breaks. Somebody watching at all times."

"Will do it," Ora said, touching Dillon's arm. "Don't worry, shipmate."

"Yall can be sure," Dalla said. "Our crews will feed and relieve us."

"Alarms!" Dillon said. "We can set up alarms with the robots!"

"Loud alarms," Ora said.

"Aye, but let's not count on the alarms. Still have to always monitor," insisted light-coloured Zimeh Bazine, a young herm from Rosebud wearing a T-shirt over small breasts and short shorts. Zee was a home-study student of engineering, not wishing to give up farming, even if only for a little while, to attend an engineering college.

The group settled their arrangements and re-assembled the 'front porch.' They did not turn off their partnership's Farm-Shield with their remotes until the Yellowood communards, dogs and humans— who had the furthest to walk to shelter from the rain — were safely back on board their Earthship®.

The animal specialists of both partnerships (Yellowood and Rosebud) prepared to move their non-human friends from their cob-buildings — outside the area of the hemispheric FarmShield — to under temporary canopies in the Shield area to the east and west of their Earthships®.

Dillon Ness stood in Yellowood's greenhouse corridor scratching behind the ears of the German shepherd named Greta, a special friend of his, watching the rain with satisfaction for several minutes until he and Greta went to take their turn — remote in hand — at monitoring the robo-cams. In Rosebud Earthship®, Dalla Dighton did the same.

▼

George W.C. Healy typed on the keyboard under the large 2D screen, until he got Yellowood Farm's robocams east to Kansas City to follow the Invaders.

The Invaders' tanks — presenting a low profile to make them harder to hit — with their mobile, steel shell cannons and flame throwers, were laying waste to the countryside formerly known as Missouri, in the low rolling landscape east of Kansas City, obliterating unprotected out-buildings, burning fields and greenbelt forests, killing all humans caught outside the EnergyShields. The Yellowood communards watched with shock and horror.

7

▼

THE INVADERS

On the Invaders' starship, the Colonels were furious their weapons could not penetrate the Energy Shields. In an empty 'community hall' just below the inner surface of the starship's lumen — their War Room — they gathered to discuss the situation:

"Nailed it, Billings," the Moderator said. "All the soldiers need do is bring us the women."

"Not the dark ones, though. Don't need no damned, savage, darkie sons," one of the youngest colonels snarled.

"Where did the Earther Losers get the EnergyShields?" Another asked.

"Our ancestors invented them," said one.

"No, their tame scientists did," said another Colonel, a man known to be more interested in precise, objective truth than in military tactics. "That's why our progenitors survived the Nuclear War," he said smugly. The rest of the Colonels despised him, but the Generals back on Faraday had made him an irrevocable part of the tactical staff, so what could they do?

"Our ancestors left that technology behind, being so damned anxious to leave Earth?" asked an irritating Colonel who questioned everything.

"Yes," the Moderator said. "The Earthers obviously broke into the Citadels and stole the Shield-technology after our ancestors left."

"So the losers aren't huddled safe in their cities, but —"

Colonel Billings said, "The cities are radioactive —"

"After *fifteen hundred* years?!!!" asked the Colonel who, again, questioned everything.

"Will be, for billions of years. Idiot," said the Colonel interested in objective truth. "The half-life of Uranium is over four billion years."

"But—"

"At least, with the EnergyShields blocking the old nukes' radiation, the Earthers probably haven't added any negative mutations to their genomes," Billings continued.

"Good for us. The women will be clean," another Colonel said.

"The *white* women," the Moderator said.

"If there are *really* any left," snapped the questioning Colonel.

"We don't have to worry. I'm sure enough of them are white enough. And in the future, we can get rid of any darkie babies—and their mothers—as soon as they're born. Easy," the youngest Colonel snarled.

"Okay, so how'll we capture enough women?" another asked.

"Sherman's March through Georgia—" a grizzled old colonel said.

"Seminov's Assault on Vega Eight!" another shouted.

A tech from Communications ran into the room, panting.

"Umm," the Moderator leaned over to listen to the tech who whispered to him. He then reported: "We have reports from several of the units who have ranged on from the cities. All of those weird dirt farmhouses of the Earthers are protected by EnergyShields. Even when the farmhouses are just clusters of cone-shaped tents."

"What! Every farmhouse has a Shield?" the grizzled old colonel asked, horrified.

"Nothing — besides ruined cities — down there on that damned planet but dirt farms, piss-small towns, and chaotic, undeveloped wilderness," the Colonel in charge of ground surveillance said. "No big estates. No elegant mansions. No new cities. No military bases. No *real* civilization."

"Trash. Mud people," the grizzled old colonel snapped.

"Damn them!" the youngest Colonel swore.

▼

While the Colonels held their strategy meetings, the enlisted men, when they were lucky enough to be off duty, were expected to be resting in their four-man quarters. Most of them were draftees.

Members of a secret society calling themselves the Final Clones met together in the toilet-facilities beside a sink loud with running water:

"Coming to Earth was our idea. The military had no right to get involved," the first man said quietly.

"But what can we do?" the second man asked.

"The Generals are twenty lightyears away, but the Colonels are just as blood-thirsty," a third man whispered.

"We have to get rid of them," said a fourth.

"What! How?" Second asked.

"Well, the military believes that killing people solves social problems. . .," First said.

"What? Wait!" Second gasped.

"Ding, *ding.* Ding, *ding.* Ding, *ding,*" the ship's bell rang, reaching them even in the cramped toilet-stall where they were meeting.

"Six bells. I've got to go on watch," the fourth man said, squeezing past to open the door.

The first man turned to the second. "Think about it." He turned off the water and they all left the room.

▼

Down below, on the part of Earth formerly called Missouri, near the confluence of the Kansas and Missouri rivers, outside of Kansas City and its western suburbs, Master Sergeant Keith Richardson — near the impregnable edge of the EnergyShield — commanded one of the sturdy tanks assigned to his squad. It was a "mini"-tank, Only eight feet tall, to present a low profile to enemy fire, measuring only twelve by thirty-three feet, with seven wheels moved by caterpillar treads. It was very tough, made of an Osmium / Iridium alloy much harder than steel or even titanium. Since there was no effective violent response yet to the invasion, Richardson was sitting on top of the tank, rather than inside, which was cramped and stuffy, as usual for tanks of all sorts ever since they had been invented in 1916. The driver and the man who loaded the munitions had to be inside to do their jobs. But Richardson didn't. He was personally in charge of applying steel-shell cannon-fire and a flame thrower to the undefended countryside west of Kansas City. On his right and left flanks, other tanks were spread out, more than a mile apart, similarly ravaging the countryside. The Faradayan soldiers were using old-fashioned weapons because their generals back on Faraday had believed steel-shells, flamethrowers, and the threat of nuclear attack would be a greater — and a more immediate — psychological terror for the Earthers than lasers and aggressively carnivorous bacteria, the usual modern weapons used to terrorize civilian populations.

Since the Earthers weren't fighting back, the Master Sergeant felt relatively safe, able to make his own observations into his throat mike for storage on the small battle recorder he carried. He intended to return to Faraday and write a bestselling book about the Invasion and its triumph.

"The Earthers have definitely de-evolved," Richardson sub-vocalized into the mike taped to his throat. "No surprise. Our ancestors — white, dynamic, and smart — left behind all the damned Darkie Losers, and—"

"Sergeant," his radio crackled.

"Yes, Sir!"

"A chopper shuttle will land near you. Send up all the het-men you can spare. We'll need them to subdue any women we capture. You know fucking demeans women, as it doesn't us, because women don't have a dick, and can't reciprocate. Over."

"Right. Yes, Sir . . . Worthington!" he shouted down to Tom inside the tank. "Off your lazy ass and get up here now!"

▼

The Sergeant continued his verbal notes a few minutes later: "The Earth was a mess from the Final Nuclear War. Played out. The Losers were left with no resources, so it's strange they could even keep farms running to feed some of them. Wonder how they decided who would eat and who would die? Obviously, they had no qualified Elites to make those kinds of decisions for them.

"Funny they've no soldiers to fight back against us," he continued. "Maybe all the soldiers died fifteen hundred years ago. But . . . soldiers can always use their weapons to get food. How else?" As a career soldier, Richardson saw his weapons as the creators of everything.

Rotating the turret of the tank, he applied steel-shelled cannon fire to an odd looking structure off to his left, easily blowing it apart. No peasants inside. Nor animals. It had obviously been made of mud, dirt, weak concrete, aluminum soda-cans, glass, cardboard, and old rubber tires (still cluttering all the Earth after an explosion of vulcanization in the twentieth, twenty-first, and the first half of the twenty-second century). *Garbage*, Richardson thought contemptuously. (He had laid bare the re-cycled building blocks of that wonderful twentieth century invention by eco-architect Michael Reynolds, the passive-solar, heavily insulated, off-the-grid Earthship®.)

"Peasants!" Richardson snarled into his battle recorder. "Nothing left on Earth to build with except dirt, junk, and trash. So this is what the dregs on Earth have become, after our ancestors left them, taking away the brightest, and the bravest . . . Leaving the Losers to waddle in filth. Primitive agricul—"

"Sergeant!" his earphones crackled again. "Up ahead of you, at two o'clock, a group of people working a farm field or something. All men, mostly darkies. No women. Don't miss the chance to kill them all. Burn the field too. Over."

"Yes, Sir!"

▼

As he obeyed orders, killing every Earther he could reach with his primitive weapons and burning the crops, the Sergeant never considered that he and his commanding officers were missing a chance to capture some actual women, because all the humans he killed—mostly dark skinned, a few sort-of pale—were dressed alike, in canvas workpants, cotton teeshirts or loose work shirts, and often straw hats. It was a cool morning there in Missouri, and none of the Earthers had their shirts off yet, which might have suggested their gender. The Sergeant and the watchers from near-Earth orbit could not see women 'dressed like men,' because women were always supposed to dress sexily to please men. (That much the men of Faraday had remembered for fifteen centuries.) Women as people who dressed to suit the work they were doing—or to please themselves in any situation—was never a concept the Faradayans could understand. They couldn't see the herms either, and wouldn't have understood their humanity.

▼

Sergeant Richardson was personally disappointed he could not continue his truncated slaughter of Earth's population. The Colonels — mindful their supply line was 19.9 lightyears long — soon stopped him from wasting armaments on unimportant, uninhabited targets. The Earth held no obvious administrative buildings nor centers of trade. No military bases could be seen from surveillance satellites in orbit. How could the Faradayans conduct a war when there was no government to attack, no centers of power to obliterate?

8

▼

PEASANT-EARTH

The 19 year old twins —Suzie and Manda Dighton—slept-in the day after their farewell party. They ignored first-bells while different Workers milked cows with Lizzy and made breakfast with Bekky. Then they rose with everyone else at second-bells and ate their breakfasts, the last Yellowood meal they would eat for at least three years.

The twins left the farm early, before the Global NewsServices came on the 2D and tiny robocams in flight reported—to all the farms and villages of Earth—the Invaders' initial attacks on the old radioactive city-ruins under their EnergyShields.

▼

After all the Yellowood communards had hugged and kissed them goodbye once again — especially their Primary Parents Bob-&-Dillon — Suzie and Manda had set off side by side on their new bicycles westward on K-96 toward Dighton Village. They had been expected to split up for their youth trips and ride off in different directions, but they were accustomed to being always in one accord, like real twins. They were determined to travel, take lovers, and live together their entire lives. They hadn't discussed their desires with the older Yellowood communards because they had wanted to avoid useless arguments about what they fully intended to do. That had been the first adult decision of their young lives. Whether or not they traveled alone or in familiar company, or didn't travel at all, was entirely their own choice. There were no laws.

After pedaling for less than an hour, they stayed on K-96 (Long Street) and pedaled right through the village to the Dighton Airstrip just west of the village, turning north on 11ᵗʰ Street and pedaling three blocks until they reached the Annabella AirStation, where they had reservations to board a solar-plane flying eastward to the Ohiyo River Valley that morning.

The plane was made of well-seasoned technology: an 80 foot long, windowless, carbon-fibre fuselage 30 feet in diameter, with a wingspan of 250 feet. There were over 18,000 perovskite photovoltaic cells covering the top of the wings, fuselage and tail. It had four electric motors, each operating a 15 foot-span propeller providing 22HP apiece from the lithium /gadolinium /niobium batteries charged by the photovoltaic cells.

Several of their teen-school classmates—wearing small backpaks— were gathered at the airstation to start their own youth trips. Like the twins, they were all Dightons, having been born from replicant-wombs in the Dighton Village BirthHouse. None of them had ever before left that region where they had been raised on various farms.

The 'twins' called to two dark young men they both found attractive: "Didier! João!" The youngsters' first names reflected that part of the Earth their genetic ancestors had come from. "Janna! Nneka! Nigel! Atara! Singh! Bob!" the 'twins' called to others.

"We're off to the Blue Ridge Mountains in the east. How bout yall?" asked Gerritt, a mahogany coloured young man. His arm was around Sook, a light brown woman of partial Korean ancestry who was known to be his long-time lover.

"Suzie, Manda, come sit with us. The boys are too rowdy today," a brown young woman, Putih Dighton, said, standing close beside a petite dark-brown woman, her lover Frida.

"Come sit with us," said Jang, a golden-skinned young man with sparkling black eyes. He was standing with Didier and João.

"Woo!" Susie said. "We were never this popular in teen school."

▼

Once the fourteen young passengers were all on board, they sprawled on the padded wool carpet of the plane's interior. Their folded bicycles were clasped out of the way along the sides of the fuselage. The pilot, Gagan Alexander — a medium-dark, middle aged woman, her tightly-curled black hair crowned with a captain's hat — taxied around and took off, speeding south on the smooth asphalt runway until the plane lifted into the air and she made a partial U-turn to fly northeast at 32,000 feet toward Ripley Village in the Ohiyo Valley, about a thousand miles away. (The people of North America had returned to the original indigenous name of that river — *Ohiyo* — called *'Beautiful River'* by the Seneca.)

The trip took over three hours in the long sunlight of summer. As the flight began — while the auto pilot was being tended by the copilot in training, Kim Scott, who was temporarily wearing the Captain's hat — Gagan joined the passengers for a delicious vegetarian lunch: a selection of cold vegetables, gazpacho, triangles of grilled cheese sandwiches on fresh baked, sourdough nutbread, a spicy casserole of whole-grain rice and red beans, and flaky fruit tarts for dessert. Food in flight was routinely catered as serve-yourself vegetarian by the AirTravel Syndic which trained the pilots, maintained the planet's airplanes, helium blimps, and airstations, and cared for all air-passengers while they traveled. Gagan took a plate in to Kim in the cockpit.

▼

Gagan came back into the fuselage and told the passengers: "We're being invaded!"

"What?" Frida said. The others echoed her.

"It's on the 2D," Gagan said.

"Aliens from outer space?" Gerritt asked. "Like old sci-fi films?"

"Like when the white-dominated, industrial nations invaded," Frida asked, "forcibly colonizing the so called *'Third World'* back in the Elite Ages?"

Gagan clicked on the 2D beside the door into the cockpit. "Let's watch here," she said. Everyone looked to the screen.

"They're wasting their time," Jang said, nibbling a carrot.

"The Shields holding?" Nneka asked, sandwich in hand.

"Aye, uh course," Gagan said. "Question is, who and what are the invaders?"

"Humanoid," Nigel said, pointing to the 2D robo-cam showing footage of soldiers floundering atop the surface of an EnergyShield over radioactive Reykjavik.

"Can we still take our YouthTrips?" Singh asked, tying back hir jet-black hair.

"I think the Invaders will waste their time trying to 'conquer' the cities, and we will all be safe in the countryside, just as our ancestors were during the Final War fifteen hundred years ago," Bob said.

"We'll be changing course slightly to avoid any Invaders our robo-cams detect," Gagan said. She had already given Kim instructions.

Fifteen centuries of total peace in the global Solidarity had skewed Earth people's understanding of how vicious any human invaders could be, so all the youngsters were confident and unafraid to continue their youth trips. None of them knew anything about — nor could they imagine the fearful viciousness of — Racism.

▼

After three hours of careful flying, Kim — under the watchful eye of Gagan — landed the plane at Ohiyo River AirStation #5 outside the Village of Ripley.

In the courtyard of the cob-hostel where the young people finally bedded down, there was a statue of Harriet 'Moses' Tubman (1820(?) to 1913), holding her ubiquitous pistol, her other hand outstretched, beaconing her passengers onward, her strong, kind face clear and determined. 'Moses' — as she had been known to many people in the nineteenth century, including the great writer and abolitionist Frederick Douglas, and of course her passengers on the Underground Railroad — was one of the most reverently remembered heroes from the era before their own, which the people of the thirty-seventh century collectively called 'The Hard Times Under the Elites', that is, *the Elite Ages*.

No one needed to imagine the awesome courage it took for someone who had just escaped from the horrors of slavery — as Tubman had — to go back into Maryland, a slave state of the USA, and bring many others — including strangers as well as her family members

— north to freedom. The people of Earth had the Black Moses, a woman of great valor. The statue in the hostel's courtyard was one of many scattered throughout the eastern part of the North American Continent, from Prince Edward Island — encircled by dikes built to Dutch specifications, reinforced by EnergyShields — to the southern tip of what was left of the Florida Peninsula.

The Village of Ripley in Brown County — sprawled along the northern side of the Ohiyo River — looked much the same as it had looked for eighteen centuries since Slavery Times, when the Village had been a major stop on the Underground Railroad. The John Rankin House — a wood-clapboard, carefully preserved, long-outdated architectural style — still crowned the highest hill overlooking the river. A plaque explained how Rankin, his wife and children had kept a candle burning in a window every night to guide escaping slaves across the Ohiyo River to freedom.

▼

The next morning, Suzie and Manda ate a hearty breakfast at the Ripley Travelers'Hostel, sharing travel plans with their Dighton classmates and other young travelers.

"We're flying to Hopewell Village behind the Energy-Screened dikes in Mercer County on the Atlantic coast to sail for the European subcontinent Sunday on the ClipperShip **Peregrine**. We'll be auxiliary crew," one olive-skinned young woman with a full jet-black afro and bright black eyes excitedly told the breakfast table.

"Really? Are there people who only sail ClipperShips? They don't farm?" a dark, chubby, young man with a bushy mustache asked.

"Aye," the young woman answered. She was wearing a bright yellow T-shirt and blue canvas shorts. "Less than ninety percent of us worldwide are needed to keep the farms operating, to feed us all. The rest run universities and hospitals, teach, do scientific research, staff factories, or—like the travel syndics—are involved in the continuous transportation of goods and people."

"We're going to *Nova Florenco Vilago*" [New Florence Village, in *Esperanto*], "on the Italian Peninsula, in the mountains, to see the Great

Art they long ago rescued from the radioactive rubble of the old cities," said another young person with medium-brown skin.

"Ah, Michelangelo," another sighed.

"Savage; Walker."

"Oh! Botticelli."

"Vermeer; Van Gogh."

"Chicago; Modersohn-Becker."

"Before we go to Europe — starting with Iceland — Manda and I are going to bicycle south to Marengo County, just north of the Caribbean, to see the Intentional Ethnic Community there — Jewish — because my genetic mother was Jewish," Suzie told everyone.

"How'd you get out there with us on the Great Plains?" Gerritt Dighton asked.

"I think my eggmother was on her YouthTrip. Common enough," Suzie answered.

"And since we're twins, we want to stay together," Manda added.

"Identical or *sororal* [*'fraternal'*]?" a tall, dark-brown young woman asked.

"Neither," Manda answered. "We've been best friends since we were decanted on the same day, grew up on the same farm, used the same bedroom, and had the same Primary Parents. Everyone always called us 'the twins.'"

"Both of us," Suzie said, "accepted that joking reference by our shipmates, friends, and classmates that we are twins, and we grew up happily feeling like it's true."

The older teens continued their breakfast, excitedly sharing all their plans for enlightening world travel on their traditional YouthTrips. They cautioned each other to keep their eTabbs handy, in case the Invaders were seen in their area and they needed to be informed to take shelter immediately under an EnergyShield in a village or on a farm.

▼

Suzie and Manda started their bicycle trip immediately after breakfast. They cycled south, west of the Appalachian Mountains, through the former states of Kentucky, then Tennessee and Alabama. The roads detoured around radioactive Lexington, Knoxville, Huntsville, Chattanooga, Birmingham, Montgomery, and others, harmless under the hemispheres of their EnergyShields. The land beneath the essentially local two-lane asphalt roads was alternately flat and rolling. Accustomed to the always flat-*flat* Kansas landscape of Lane County, the girls found they had to strengthen their muscles to cycle up many of the slight hills the road flowed over. Then they could enjoy relaxing and laughing together with delight, letting gravity take over on the downhill glides.

They slept at night outdoors under the stars on the emerald grass beside the road, after opening a small, easy-up, dome tent they could use in case it rained. Travelers all over the Earth often did that. People sleeping on the roadsides in good weather was not from homelessness, but rather because everyone felt that every Person on Earth *owned* the Earth, *deserved* the Earth, *belonged* to the Earth, and could use it as their *'private property'*, as long as they did not interfere with the needs of communal land management. The sides of local highways — there were no 'federal', 'state', or 'regional' highways — were customarily kept green-grassy, clean, and useful for everyone for sleeping or picnicking.

▼

When they passed through villages, they renewed their travel-food stores and treated themselves to 'fancy food' at the Village Cafeteria. It was also a chance to shower, wash their clothes, sleep in a soft bed at the Village Travelers' Hostel, and meet other young people for conversation, games, or sex.

Mostly, the trip to re-discover Suzie's genetic past at a Jewish Intentional Ethnic Community was a chance for the two girls to spend time alone together, enjoying their *twin*-hood. Even though they were young, they were both happy to know they would be together their whole lives, like real twins would be, they believed.

They often joked, as they lay side by side on their backs at night — viewing the stars above and the steadily moving lights of Earth's communication satellites — that it was a shame they were not Lesbians, or bisexual, so they could have more sex as they traveled, (since they loved each other), and then would not have to rely on chance heterosexual encounters with young men at the occasional Travelers' Hostel. They had each, of course — from the age of thirteen onward — explored their own sexuality with boys their own age in and around the farms of Lane County in the Dighton area, and had compared notes with each other at night in their mutual bedroom. Neither of them had ever had more than brief encounters with sex play and were now ready to think of settling down to a longer and more intense sexual relationship when it should come about for one or both of them.

Their trip south took nearly three months—three happy, safe, free, fulfilling months when their strengthened *twin*-bond was made even more unique and precious to both of them, until they felt the nip of autumn in the air some nights as they luxuriated under the stars on the roadside grass in their sleepsaks.

▼

Suzie and Manda were in the area formerly known as southwestern Alabama—not far from their goal in Marengo County, standing thigh deep in a narrow, swift running creek — (the eTabb mapmaker collective had forgotten to record its name) — leading to the Tombigbee River. They were naked, laughing, splashing, bathing, not at all fearful of any danger from wild animals since they were in farm country not wilderness, and also not fearful — as naked women — of any danger from other human beings.

That danger, they knew, had been common in earlier ages, but did not exist in their world. The post-Elite, non-competitive, non-racist, sexually-free anarchist society into which the twins had been born had been a worldwide, nonviolent, *non-sexist* Solidarity for over fifteen hundred years. While they bathed, their bicycles, clothes, backpaks, and eTabbs were waiting for them on the bank beside the creek.

As they laughingly splashed each other, water droplets sparkled in the sunlight like diamonds, decorating and enhancing the joy of their afternoon bath.

A winged vehicle spewing noxious gases landed in a field near them, wantonly crushing the food plants. Three men in strange identical outfits jumped out of the vehicle and ran toward the girls, wading into the creek.

"Hey, Folks!" Suzie called to them. ""Yall don't need to get yall's clothes wet —"

One man lifted an ugly mass of metal and riddled dark-skinned Suzie with steel bullets. She collapsed, bloody, into the water as two of the men grabbed Manda, who was much paler of skin. "What? What're yall doing? Suzie! *Suzie!*" Manda screamed.

Suzie Dighton began to float downstream, bleeding, wounded, her arms flailing, struggling against the force of the current. Spewing blood, she gasped out, "*Manda.*"

The uniformed man calmly fired more bullets. The shots were loud.

"*Suzie! No!*" Manda howled in horror.

With no break in the surprise of the savagery, Suzie drifted swiftly away, her dead eyes staring, the water around her soon blood-free as her ruined heart stopped beating.

"*Suzie! Suzie!*" Manda continued to scream, sobbing, terror stricken, frantically struggling to free herself from the strangers holding her. She was shocked by the violence, the barbarity — long missing from the Earth — the first she had seen in all her young life. Manda yearned toward her twin, twisting in her captivity to keep Suzie — *Suzie!* — in sight as she floated quickly away, dark and dead.

Then Manda was alone with her captors. Truly alone without her twin for the first time in her life.

9

—————— ▼ ——————

THE INVADERS

Tom Worthington and a few other het-men were flown to an Invaders' surveillance satellite in geosynchronous orbit above the radioactive ruins of Nairobi on the eastern African continent. Tom, who had a small-plane pilot's license on Faraday, spent his flight time in the cockpit, quizzing the pilots on the spaceplane's operation.

Tom hated being a soldier. Preparing to kill people — even Earthers who were not *his* people — had never been the way he wanted to spend his life. On Faraday, Tom had achieved what he wanted: a quiet academic position lecturing in a subject which greatly interested him. Knowing it was not safe to express his hatred of the military lifestyle with anyone other than his friend Bill, Tom continually seethed with rage, hiding his true feelings from the other men around him, especially his officers.

Because his father had become a successful small businessman, and was thus reasonably affluent, Tom had been able to afford to spend his young adult days learning at a university. He was, after all, the youngest clone-son of four — sufficiently non-macho enough that he was presumed to be damaged by replicative-fading — and was never expected to follow his father into business. As a reasonably well-paid professor — which he had always wanted to be — he was happy to think of spending his life teaching and researching Anthropology, studying how human beings relate to one another culturally. He had made friends with Bill (William Richard McClevy) when inquiring into Earth history, Doctor McClevy's area of expertise. Tom knew anthropology cannot be studied without looking at the multitude of ways human beings in various situations in former times on the natal planet had coped with the problems of humans living and working together.

The Colonels in charge of the Invasion had called for het-men to subdue the women who were captured. At least Tom wouldn't be told to kill them. Women would be of no use solving Faraday's reproduction-problem if they were dead, he believed. But Tom couldn't think of intercourse with a woman as 'subduing' her. His template for possible sex with a real woman had always been what his friend Bill had told him of homosexual encounters: *a sharing between equals of the physical pleasure and spiritual joy of sexual intimacy.*

Tom had always thought that if women were human beings, not brainless automatons like robots — and they would have to be human beings, or men could not productively breed with them — then why would heterosexual sex be qualitatively, socially, anthropologically different from the homosexual experiences Bill had always told Tom he enjoyed? Provided a man was not xenophobic. . . .

These thoughts whirled through Tom's head as he gathered on the satellite with a few other het-men for instructions from a Sergeant before they were sent into the captured women.

"Boys, this is the chance we het-men have been praying for all our lives."

That's certainly true, Tom thought.

"Once we take the women, once they experience real sex with real men—not those Loser males down there on Earth— then they are subdued, truly owned, and they belong to us, to Faraday. We won't have any trouble at all with them afterwards."

I wonder if that's true, Tom thought.

▼

The small satellite in orbit above Nairobi was not designed to spin to give the crew 'artificial gravity.' The satellite was there to facilitate close, constant observation of the Earth's surface. Eleven others were spaced equally around the equator, in geosynchronous orbit, more than twenty-two thousand miles above sea level.

To prevent debilitating loss of calcium from their bones—caused by prolonged exposure to free fall—crews were rotated regularly back to the main starship spinning at Lagrange Point **L2** behind the Moon almost a million miles from Earth.

The 'Mission Briefing' took place in free fall, the only condition of having been snatched from the surface of Faraday into Space which Tom found he enjoyed. *'Mission Briefing', Ha!* Tom thought, *As if having sex with a woman were an Act of War!*

After the briefing, giddy with the pleasure of once again experiencing free fall, Tom jaunted along toward the compartment where the woman was being kept whom he was assigned to 'subdue'.

▼

Manda was forbidden any clothing and carefully parked floating naked in free fall in the middle of the cubed-shaped compartment where she was confined. She was unable to touch any of the six 'walls' and push against them to adjust her position. She had heard about free fall, but had never experienced it. She was utterly helpless, and felt tense, nauseous, frantic with the continual sensation of falling, unable to grasp anything solid. She was still mourning Suzie. Her grief was so strong it nearly overcame her fear.

Tom opened the hatch, saw Manda—naked—and pushed off, slowly, toward her, intending to bring them both gently against the padded 'wall' opposite the hatch.

Manda fought him when he reached her. She was ineffective, having had no self-defense training, since life on PeasantEarth in 3683 — in terms of attack from another human being — was never dangerous, for anyone. On Earth, it was a proud, common custom of manhood for a man never to be violent in any way toward anyone — a child, a woman, an elder, a handicapped person, or otherwise — who was not as strong as himself.

However, Tom from the planet Faraday was a soldier trained in effective violence. He confined himself to holding Manda immobile, incapable of struggling further, even though she was amazingly strong. He looked into her eyes.

Unlike a robot, hers were not dead eyes. They were ablaze with rage and fear. Still struggling, they reached the padded wall. Tom stopped them from bouncing by grabbing a strap. He held her firmly with his other arm.

"Hello," he said, smiling at her. "My name's Tom Worthington. What's yours?"

Manda exploded in fury again, terrified, screaming. She was naked and he was wearing clothes, a uniform identical to that worn by the monsters who had killed Suzie.

Tom fought to calm her. "Hey, it's okay. I won't hurt you. It'll be okay," he said, comprehending she didn't believe him. He wasn't sure he believed himself. But he realized it would be impossible for him to have pleasant, human-to-human sex with a woman in her emotional state. Which he could do nothing about.

"Murderer!" she shrieked, flailing at him.

"What!"

"You killed my twin! You killed her! *Suzie!*" She sobbed. Gobs of tears appeared over her eyes. In free fall, there was no down, no gravitational pull to draw the salt water away from its source. Clumsy, unable to see clearly, she swiped at the tears with her hands, setting herself and Tom spinning erratically together next to the padded surface. Bumping against it, they started to drift, still spinning, away from the wall, accompanied by small, perfectly-spherical globes of hazy salt-water.

"Oh, I'm sorry. I didn't kill anyone," Tom sputtered. Despite her obvious lack of a penis, he spoke to her as if she were an actual human being. (His xenophobic '*instincts*' were weak, an obvious result of replicative-fading.)

Her body was not hairless nor dressed like the sexual robots familiar to him. He had no sexual desire, just concern for her as a distressed person. His instructors in Basic Training would have been ashamed to see how they had failed to make him over into a '*good*' soldier, merciless with '*the enemy*'.

"Suzie! Suzie!" Sensing his genuine concern and innate gentleness, Manda clutched at Tom for comfort, sobbing her unbearable grief. As a member of Earth's peaceful, world-wide Solidarity, she was accustomed to comfort and support from other human beings, of any age or cultural-traits — men, women, herms, trans-people — never force or violence, no matter how much they disagreed.

His arms around her nude body, Tom felt a stirring of his heterosexual desire. He resolutely ignored it. He held a child in pain, not a thing with a willing, useful vagina. (Tom was not at all lacking in empathy. Because he was an imperfect clone, deficient in xenophobia, her difference did not frighten him. He saw her as a human being like himself, however oddly shaped.) "What can I do to help?" he whispered, deeply saddened. They bumped, gently, into another wall. He groped for the handy loop of a strap and twisted until they stopped spinning.

She was quiet in his arms for a long time. . . .

He despaired of any reasonable response from her until she finally whispered, "Take me home."

"What?"

"Home. . .," she whispered again, her throat tight, squeaking softly.

"Wait . . . Let me think." He had spent some time as observation crew on one of the other satellites in orbit over Earth's equator. He hoped they were all the same layout.

She started crying again.

"Okay," he said. He didn't understand his strong impulse to help her — although it seemed the only decent choice — but he was resolute. "We'll have to be furtive." He held her away from him and looked into her teary eyes. "You'll have to be very quiet. We're at war, remember? If I take you away, I'll be committing Treason, and if we're caught, they'll kill me and re-enslave you." Being a draftee, he had no feelings of loyalty toward the Faradayan Military. He carefully brushed her tears away with his free hand. Small globes of salt water again scattered in the air around them. "Understand?" he asked.

She gulped and nodded. She had been mistreated enough to understand the danger she was in, strange and alien though it was.

▼

Sneaking from alcove to storage closet. Tom rushing their frantic flight, holding her against him with one arm. She limp, silent, making no moves to tumble them in unwanted directions. No one saw them. Everyone else on the satellite was either 'subduing' other women who had been captured, or were fulfilling their duties observing the surface of Earth.

Flying in free fall, they finally reached the vehicle bay where he spied a space-plane he thought he could pilot. He grabbed a small coverall from a clasp as they jaunted past.

The plane was unlocked. Theft of military equipment was unthinkable. Inside, he handed her the coverall and helped her strap into the co-pilot's seat. He sent the radio signal from his control panel to let them pass through the EnergyField — it was there to hold a breathable atmosphere and pressure in the satellite — and they catapulted out into space. As they jetted — spewing noxious gasses — toward the surface of the Earth, Tom was surprised they hadn't been seen.

His radio, automatically tuned to Satellite Control, erupted with demands for identification and an explanation of his actions: "What is your flight plan?" He ignored it. Satellite Control had no weapons.

"Thanks for the coverall," the woman said quietly. "Umm, my name's Manda Dighton."

"Okay. Now, the satellite we just left is in orbit over the Continent of Africa. Do you understand maps? Do you know how to find your home?"

"Aye. Fly west, uh . . . *north*west, please, over the Atlantic Ocean, to the North American continent, then west over the Appalachian Mountains and the Mississippi River to the Great Plains of the continent. Do you have a map?"

"It's old, of Earth before the . . . uh, War."

"Okay. I know some history, at least of the area where I was born. We need to fly to . . . to Lane County . . . in the middle of the western half of the . . . old state of Kansas." She tapped the map displayed on the 2D screen of the plane's control panel. "Bout there. Not far past the Monument to George Washington Carver. But . . . uh . . . the Monument is not marked on your screen," she frowned.

"I'm Tom, by the way. You remember?"

"Aye. Thank you for doing this. After I attacked you."

"Well, I . . . uh, just want to help. What happened to your — you said — twin?"

Waving her hands, helpless to explain the horror of the unexpected murder, Manda began crying again. Strapped in his own seat, having to concentrate on flying an unfamiliar craft, Tom was unable to be of any help. She continued to cry, sitting alone, shaking her head, gulping air, unable to speak.

▼

Several hours later, once they crossed the Mississippi River, Manda directed him south by southwest. She asked to use the radio, called a phone-tower she knew about, and excitedly, then mournfully, spoke a strange language to someone, crying, pausing at intervals to give Tom directions in English.

They touched down easily on a runway in the flat landscape beside a small town. Tears running down her cheeks — torn between grief for Suzie and joy at returning home to her farm family where she would be guaranteed safety, love, and understanding — Manda was bouncing in her seat with excitement.

10

▼

PEASANT-EARTH

Manda opened the door on her side and leapt out before the plane had fully stopped. Stumbling, sobbing, she ran into the arms of two people in overalls standing side by side—apparently both males—who were darker-skinned than she was. They held her tight and cried with her. A small multi-coloured crowd of other Earthers came and held the trio, adding their tears.

Tom stopped the space plane and got out, walking slowly — ill at ease — back toward the group of strangers surrounding Manda.

A middle aged, nut-brown man with a mass of curly black hair—wearing dark blue overalls, a striped green shirt, and a small, round hat—left the group and approached Tom. Since the custom of shaking hands in greeting had long ago disappeared on Earth, the brown Earther put his palms together and bowed his head slightly. He said, "I'm Sheldon Rozel. Thank you for bringing Manda back to us. Was there nothing you could do to save her twin?"

"I wasn't there. I'm Tom Worthington. I understand *her . . . twin?* was too dark."

"Too dark?" Sheldon said, surprised. "Well . . . oh. . . ." Confused, anguished, he spun in place, looking up to the sky. Finally, he sighed, shaking his head. "Thank you for saving Manda for us. We'll be taking her home now. Like to come along?"

"Yes . . . uh . . . yes! I've, umm . . . committed Treason. I can't go back," Tom said. He didn't sound as sad as he was beginning to feel. "You can have the spaceplane for the war effort. I hope it helps."

"We can't use it. Needs too much refined petroleum," Sheldon answered. "Our war effort is totally defense. Thank you anyway. I imagine folks from the AirTravel Syndic will take it apart. Some of it may be useful, somehow. . . . Well, let me introduce you to the horses."

Two horses were strapped side by side in front of a large, shallow wooden box set up on four great wheels. A padded wooden bench sat in the box facing the horses. To Tom, they were great frightening beasts with shining coats and large, possibly malevolent eyes.

"This is *Monto-Flanko*, means 'Mountainside' in English," Sheldon said, affectionately patting one horse's neck. "And this," he said, rubbing the front of the other horse's head, "is *Oro-Polvo*, means 'Gold dust.' See the points of golden light scattered throughout her coat? These two — *Polvo* and *Flanko* — pull well together. Make great saddle horses too."

The one called *Flanko* leaned its head over Sheldon's shoulder and he stepped forward to embrace the horse's neck. "You can rub his muzzle, gently, if you want," he said, looking back at Tom.

"Uh, no," Tom said, stepping back nervously.

"Okay." Sheldon stepped away from *Flanko* and shouted to the other humans who were standing beside saddled horses, "Let's go!" Using the spokes of one wheel as steps, he climbed aboard the wooden box and sat on the bench, taking up some long leather straps attached somehow to the horses. "Come on up!" he called to Tom.

Feeling apprehensive and very clumsy, Tom clambered aboard the wheeled box and sat on the bench next to Sheldon.

Manda and the rest of her family mounted the saddled horses, and they rode off through the Village of Dighton leading and following Sheldon who clucked at *Polvo* and *Flanko* to get them going.

What Tom saw of Dighton was long stretches of colorfully painted one and two story buildings made of dried mud—most apparently residences—set among trees. Tom found it very primitive. Besides mud, they seemed to use a lot of glass, especially on the treeless south sides of the buildings. They went along Annabella Street through the village.

They turned right at Eagle Avenue and left at Long Street and were finally out in the countryside on a two-lane asphalt highway, which also seemed very primitive to Tom, as it had a line of low-growing greenery running down the middle of the road.

His perch on the wooden bench facing the horses' rumps seemed very unstable to Tom. *What if the animals bolt?* He clutched the side of the bench in fearful anticipation. One of the horses in front of him twitched its tail aside and extruded some feces which plopped to the road. A disgusting sight. Tom clutched the bench even harder and fought nausea as the unfamiliar odor reached him.

"Makes great fertilizer," Sheldon commented, chuckling. "Dighton Village has solar-powered robots ranging the roads and paths for sixty miles round. They process the horseshit and distribute it to every farm in bio-degradable bags. You see, we can't afford to waste any resource. Horse manure makes it extra terrific to live with horses. They process grass, hay, and grain into fertilizer. . . . Oh, as a horse whisperer, I'm clearly biased. But everybody likes horses."

"Horse whisperer? What's that?" Tom asked.

"Just means I'm extra *simpatia* with horses," he said automatically, unthinkingly using an *Esperanto* word, "although as an animal expert, I like cows, chickens, ducks, geese, cats, dogs, phoxes, and all other animals too. I've been for years trying to convince my fellow communards to put in a pond and raise ducks and —

"Ah, we need to turn in here," he interrupted himself. He pulled on the leather straps. "Pinklight Farm. Yellowood's running low on coffee." The rest of the riders continued past them on the road to their farm, escorting Manda home.

At first, as they rode alongside it, the Pinklight residence appeared to be an extensive hill covered with wildflowers. Then Sheldon drove down around to the south side which was bright with glass. They disembarked and entered the residence through a ten foot wide greenhouse, with glass overhead, filled with sunlight, prolific with plants. At the end of the greenhouse, they passed through a glass door in a tall shuttered glass wall, and found themselves in a large, cool, comfortable living / dining room with a kitchen on one side. Tall bookcases lined the side and back walls.

"Sanite!" Sheldon greeted a medium-tall, dark woman wearing blue cotton trousers with bulging cargo-pockets. She had brown eyes almond-shaped by epicanthic folds, and curly auburn hair in a loose 'fro. "Bekky called you, I think," he said. "We need coffee."

The woman was bare breasted, which upset Tom. The sight of a woman's bare breasts was in his experience exclusively a part of his sex-rec time. She was young, but obviously not a child, and her breasts stood up round and perfect, with erect nipples in the cool room. Tom bent over to hide his involuntary erection. He clenched his teeth to hold back a groan. Fortunately, Sheldon and *the almost-naked! woman* were busy talking.

"Oh! Tom, this is Sanite Spencer," Sheldon suddenly said. "Sanite, this is Tom, er . . ."

"Worthington," Tom gasped, hiding his erection from them behind the dining table.

"Nice to meet you, Tom," Sanite said. "Coffee, Sheldon, of course. Want some mangos and plantains too, won't yall? And shrooms?"

"Oh, aye."

▼

After a tour for the newcomer of the windowless Pinklight Indoor Farm under the flower-covered hill — with the flickering aspect of the pinklight turned off to ease the human eye — Tom had himself under control by the time they arrived at Yellowood Farm where the greenhouse was only a wide corridor bursting with plants, and the larger garden was outside. He was introduced to several people, including a very attractive, tan-skinned, young adult woman with slanted hazel eyes and dark reddish hair, fortunately wearing a T-shirt covering her apparently ample breasts.

"Lizzy," Bob Beiler said quietly, "your general knowledge of anthropology would be helpful in orientating this fellow to Yellowood Farm and to our world culture."

"He's a soldier. He's killed people," Lizzy snapped. "Put him out and let him go back to his Army."

"Obviously he's changed sides. He brought Manda back to us. We're grateful to him for that. If you won't show him around and explain our ways, who should I get to do it?"

Irritated, Lizzy stared at Bob. *He's always so good at managing people,* she thought, irritated. "All right. All right," she sighed. "I'm glad

Manda's back. Obviously he can't return to the Invasion-Forces. I'll do it. Ah . . . Come on, Soldier. Let me show you the farm." She walked to the shuttered door leading into the greenhouse corridor.

Following her, Tom said earnestly, "I've been lucky. I've never killed anyone. I'm only a draftee soldier. Just . . . uh . . . cannon-fodder. I'm really a senior professor of Anthropology at Clarke University in Rockefeller City on the planet Faraday. Or was," he said sadly.

"Oh?" Lizzy said, turning to him, her hand on the door handle. "Then we sort-of share some academic language. Uh, I don't suppose you speak *Esperanto*?"

"What? No."

"*Esperanto* is our global language. All children on Earth are taught it from babyhood —"

"What?" Tom mumbled again, still confused by the thoroughly alien culture he had been taught was — an extremely *primitive* postwar Earth.

"Beginning when they are babies," Lizzy said, "all children of Earth are taught to speak — and later, write — *Esperanto*. Um, as part of the learning in our teen years, everyone is taught about the panicked-flight of the Elites after the Final War, as well as the triumph of the Earth's (and its People's) Recovery."

"Recovery from the War?" Tom asked. He had always believed it was impossible to recover from a planet-wide nuclear war.

"Aye. Survivors all over the Earth," she said, "needed to communicate effectively with each other so they could — in Solidarity — most effectively share and preserve our scarce resources, neutralize the danger of radiation, consolidate our world-wide civilization, and" — taking a deep breath, she waved her arms wide, as if embracing the whole world — "share scientific discoveries, as well as feed and house everyone. Then of course our ancestors needed to begin to reproduce the next generation."

"How was that possible, with all the radiation?"

"Scientific procedures had to be developed." she continued, "to expunge the human genome of damage brought about by the high levels of radiation from the bombed cities before they were all finally quarantined by impenetrable EnergyScreens.

"So, post-Final-War science quickly developed," she said, "all over the world, the ability for 'clean' human procreation — removing damaged genes from the reproductive process — in local village BirthHouses, with technical pre-screening, and replicant-wombs, outside women's bodies. . . .

"As a young teen, each woman stores an ovary in stasis in her local BirthHouse, and the fallopian tube of the other ovary is valved-off in her body so she can still enjoy the female hormones produced by her remaining ovary. Then — and as a woman, I am particularly happy about this — all women are as free as men have always been, to enjoy their bodies in every kind of sexual encounters, even those which could have created an unwanted pregnancy in earlier times, in the Elite Ages. And in addition, venereal disease organisms — like those causing AIDS, syphilis, and gonorrhea, as well as Chlamydia, herpes, genital warts, cervical cancer, etc — were quickly made extinct in the following centuries.

"The children of those," Lizzy continued, "who had survived the Final War were the first generation of human beings to be born from replicant-wombs, carrying the best possible combinations of their genetic-parents' carefully selected, undamaged genes. They inherited a society which was collectively honest and decent enough that women and men — plus all people who were gender-fluid or non-conforming for any reason — could be in charge of themselves, without interference from anyone else, determining exactly how, as individuals, their own genetic material would be used. Thus the proud profession of BirthHouse Worker began, helping everyone to reproduce in the best and the safest way possible."

"Um, weren't there any problems from social-conservatives, particularly very religious people?" he asked.

"Aye. We are taught in our teen-school history classes that, right after the War — as scientific research and work in village BirthHouses began to produce undamaged children — traditionalist and reactionary people were horrified by the prospect of babies being grown in artificial replicant-wombs, what the ultra-conservatives called '*test tubes*.' Reactionaries believed that making babies in the BirthHouses was '*the*

Devil's Work', so they insisted on trying to reproduce *'only in the manner sanctified by God'*.

"Didn't work, I would suppose. Too much radiation damage?"

"Aye. Immediately after the Final War — by rejecting the 'liberal abomination' of scientifically creating healthy children in local BirthHouses — women with old fashioned beliefs — or those who were controlled by hetero-sexist, ultra-conservative men insisting on 'normal' ways of creating children — often died, unfortunately birthing children who were severely damaged and frequently non-viable."

"Sounds like a mess, anthropologically speaking," Tom frowned.

"Sure, but nevertheless, the ordinary people of the new global Solidarity went on to take care of the surviving, damaged children for all of their lives, because the children themselves were not at fault for the *'stubbornness'* of their genetic mothers (or fathers). Local BirthHouses were even able to help some of them reproduce using whatever genetic material they had that was undamaged.

"Grief-stricken sexual 'traditionalists'," she continued, "blamed the BirthHouses for 'their' women dying in childbirth (because God obviously was punishing *'Man'*— ha! — for rejecting the *'sanctified'*, normal, pleasuring-heterosexual-males way of making babies). In their xenophobic madness, they often attacked the BirthHouses and their Workers. But the xenophobes were outnumbered by the great numbers of ordinary people — like us, today, their descendents — with no religious or political agenda, who were willing to let science help them safely create healthy human children with the best combination of whatever genes-undamaged-by-radiation each genetic parent carried. They defended the BirthHouses, and within two generations, the problem completely disappeared."

"Woo! That's good," Tom said. He was finding the strange story fascinating.

"We have records that long ago, in the global discussions immediately after the Final War — when everyone was intoxicated with the dual sensations of local and worldwide Solidarity — human society on Earth came round to the understanding that the genuine possibility of women as free persons had always been hampered by the stark reality of a woman's fertility. Throughout most of _his_tory, an individual woman was rarely able to control her own ability to procreate."

"We were taught on Faraday that birthing babies was what God had created women _for_," Tom said.

"And sex."

"Yeah . . ." That wasn't a topic Tom wanted to talk about, because, to his surprise and discomfort, he was finding Lizzy — a living human being he could talk to — very attractive. That was something he had no experience with. "But back to _Esperanto_. . . ." he said.

"The only partially universal language our ancestors had immediately after the Final War — besides Japanese — was English, the language of past white oppressors. Those conquerors —ruled by plutocratic Elites — had, with the use of machine-guns — stolen land, lives, resources, and labor from the people of the so-called 'third world' (the _'undeveloped'_ countries).

The 'Left Behinds' had feared that 'Translators' — people who, at first, had facilitated conversations between survivors all over the bombed-out and ruined Earth — might, over time, become a separate, more powerful class, poisoning the desire of the great majority of the world's surviving Peoples to create an Egalitarian, worldwide society free of the triple scourges of Status, Privilege, and Elitism.

"So they had turned to _Esperanto_," Lizzy continued, "which incidentally had a philosophy of world peace imbedded within its structure and vocabulary. It was created in the nineteenth century by a Polish-Jewish ophthalmologist, L.L.Zamenhof. And despite Elite opposition to the idea that the common people of Earth would no longer be conveniently divided by language, _Esperanto_ had survived into the twenty-second century, living like yeast latent in the culture worldwide of ordinary people. It had therefore been extant when it was desperately needed as a global language —"

"But you speak English," Tom interrupted, "barely changed from what we speak on Faraday."

"We speak Ameriglish — as it is spoken by those born and raised on the North American Continent—which almost two thousand years ago began to be differentiated from what the English people themselves spoke."

"Okay. Why are you speaking . . . Ameri . . . glish . . . not *Esperanto?*"

"Ameriglish, fortunately for you, and for Manda, is my ethnic language."

"Ethnic? What?"

"Here in *North* America, <u>ex</u>-cluding Caribbean, Central, and South America, the general ethnic culture is WASP."

"But you're not. . . It seems —"

"WASP used to mean: white, Anglo-Saxon, Protestant, but by the mid twenty-second century — when after the devastation of the Final War, the Elites panicked and abandoned the Earth, freeing the rest of us to finally begin creating a *real* civilization —"

"I guess those Elites were my ancestors."

"Or the useful Workers they forced to go along with them. Don't insult yourself."

"What? Insult?" Tom, asked, confused by her apparently — *not admiring the Elites! Was she proud of being a peasant?* (In his Faradayan mind, peasants were vastly ignorant, physically dirty, the lowest of the low. Barely human. Sub-human.)

"Before the damned Elites left the Earth," Lizzy doggedly continued — (Apparently she *was proud* to be a peasant*!*) — "the general WASP culture in North America had been enlarged and diversified to include the mixed-colour descendants of kidnapped Africans. Enslaved Black African women had been routinely raped by their owners, supposedly for breeding purposes to '*improve*' the stock," Lizzy snarled.

She continued, "So-called-WASP culture in North America also came to include as well: the surviving remnant of indigenous North American tribal people; as well as non-white immigrants from south of the RioGrande; the 'not-white-enough' eastern European and Asian immigrants; Liberal-Protestants, Catholics, Jews, Muslims, Bahá'í, and Atheists; adherents to home grown religions; and small insular societies experimenting with diverse new ways of living together. Since then, we have still labeled the culture 'WASP', even though nowadays people make no effort to keep genes for 'white' skin-colour isolated, since melanin in human skin is a great protection against damage from sunlight. And we like the wonderful variety of the colour."

"Oh," he mumbled.

"Religious belief is very personal," she continued, "taking group-form only on individual farms sometimes, or within Intentional Ethnic Communities — like all kinds of NativeAmerican cultures, and various Mexican, Jewish, Bahá'í, or Muslim cultures, diverse Christian sects, Amish, or . . . er, Mennonite — inside our larger North American-continental so-called-WASP culture. . . ."

"Um . . . so I am now in a WASP ethnic area? Even though no one — well, only one person — here really looks white to me?"

"I explained bout the enlarged and diversified," Lizzy snarled, frowning. "On the North American continent, we have people with genetics from all over the world —"

"Why are so few of you white . . . uh, very pale-skinned?"

"Because through all of Earth's history most human beings on Earth weren't white, or pale skinned," Lizzy snapped. "That was true long before the Final War. Now, with our custom of everybody taking a YouthTrip after teen-school, meeting people from many different historical-cultures, and often choosing to reproduce with them, we've found that if someone wants a child with really pale skin, the techs at a BirthHouse must be careful to select for the embryo a full set of recessive genes for very little melanin from each donor, sometimes more than two. Three is common, I understand, when it comes to selecting for very pale skin-colour.

"Our Bekky Shields, Yellowood Farm's food-cord, is very pale, I'm sure you've noticed," Lizzy said, gesturing toward her shipmate seated at the food preparation table chopping rhubarb. "Her three genetic donors—on their YouthTrips, they got together on the farm where she grew up—wanted to create a child who was unusual looking, so they asked the techs to select all their genes producing very low melanin, much less than most people. "Bekky?" she asked her shipmate. "What farm did you grow up on? I forget."

"Nuts'n'Berries," Bekky answered, smiling. "'Where long life begins'."

"Ha," Lizzy laughed. "Are all your genetic parents still there?"

"One of my Moms is. Dad and my other Mom left when I was ten. Moved to the California Islands. Great place to vacation. I manage to go about once a year. My othermother taught me how to sail a small boat."

"So your childhood farm produces those dark-colored berries we all love to eat for a healthy old age?"

Aye," Bekky said. "We were a regular farm in every other way. Goats, chickens, an ordinary Earthship®, lots of melons in the garden, besides the berry bushes. Only one cow. That's why I moved to Yellowood. I like cows. Funny, useful animals."

11

▼

PEASANT-EARTH

"So, Tom, there you have it," Lizzy said, leading Tom outside through the sunny greenhouse corridor and out the south door into the south garden. "Here in North America, like in most of the world, in WASP culture, we like diversity, in people, food, religion —"

"And so some of you, um . . . aren't Christians?"

"I don't know, actually. Religion is a private matter. Here at Yellowood, we practice privacy, but we *do* follow some communal Pagan customs together with other farmers in the area, dancing with African /Indigenous drums on the Solstice — naked only in the summer, of course —"

"Naked?. . . Ah . . . umm . . . Pagans? So, you believe in multiple Gods?"

"I suppose some—but not all—Pagans do, and Christians have three gods. Or is it two? Although they deny it. . . . But most Theists believe in only one God. Or Goddess. And of course many people are Atheists. The Pagan dancing is fun, though. I love the drums. And sometimes we celebrate Passover dinner here at Yellowood with Sheldon, who's Jewish, or Cinco de Mayo at Rosebud Farm, with Juana Guadalupe, who's Mexican, or Easter egg hunts—"

"Tell me, uh . . . about this building here," Tom interrupted. They had reached the cob-barn. Like the Earthship®, it appeared to be built of mud, colorfully painted in fanciful bas-relief designs. Its building material (cob) was a mixture of water, sand, clay, and straw sculpted into a pleasing shape with round corners. The overhanging roof was covered with a variety of greenery.

"Vegetables, herbs," Lizzy told him when he asked about the roof. "This is the building where we of Yellowood Farm house our animal friends, the horses, the cows, and" — she said, pointing to an area mostly outside — "the chickens, over there, under those Mulberry trees. This barn is where the cats, phoxes, and dogs bunk too, unless they're buddies with a specific human, and sleep with them in the Earthship®. Can you ride a horse?"

"No, uh . . . I told, um . . . Sheldon — we have no horses on Faraday."

"Oh . . . Well, I'll put you on a horse, so we can explore the farm."

"But I don't know how to steer a horse —"

"All you'll have to do is sit. I'll lead you. Here." Escorted by two Jack Russell terriers, she opened a stall door, encouraging the piebald horse within to back up and make room for the humans. A black cat jumped off the horse's back onto the top of a partition between the stalls. Licking a paw, zee stared down at the humans and hissed briefly at the dogs, who ignored hir.

Tom was uneasy to be in a confined space with the huge animal which seemed to have a dozen long legs with hard, sharp feet. Dogs underfoot, the stall seemed very crowded. The body odor of the horse, not unpleasant, filled the stall.

"This is Two Socks," Lizzy said, affectionately patting the side of the horse's neck. "See the white sock pattern on two opposite corner feet, but not the other two?"

Tom bravely looked the great beast in the eye. It seemed to be — amazingly — a gentle individual. "Uh, yes," he said, glancing at the legs. There *did* appear to be two — and only two — socked feet.

Lifting a mass of leather off a wooden trolley, Lizzy said, "And this is Two Sock's saddle. Each horse has hir own fitted saddle." After putting a small blanket on, she put the saddle on the horse's back and proceeded to cinch it with a belt under its belly. Then she pulled on the saddle, presumably to check if it was on tight. She leaned down and patted the horse's under belly. "Now, Two Socks, you know I don't like to punch you. Let out the air. Please." She continued patting the horse's rounded belly. The horse turned its head and looked at Lizzy, then whooshed out its breath and whinnied, tossing its head. Lizzy quickly cinched the belt tighter, then added a second.

"Okay, just another minute," Lizzy said. She urged Tom out of the stall, and closed the door on the saddled horse.

She opened another stall door and went inside to saddle the horse, then brought it out. It was a magnificent creature, hir coat shiny and jet black, eyes bright. "This is my personal favorite of the farm's horses— Nokto, we call her, short for Noktomezo, *Esperanto* for 'Midnight.'" Lizzy explained to Tom. "She's a good horse, ain't you girl?" She caressed the horse on its muzzle.

Tom was amazed at the warm relationship Lizzy had with the horses.

▼

Lizzy brought out Two Socks while Nokto stood and waited.

"Okay, Tom, come here. No, the left side, always the *left* side of a horse. It's how they're trained. Okay. This is the stirrup. Put your left foot into it and swing your right leg over"—"Easy girl, easy," she said to Two socks—"Okay, you can let your butt down and sit in the saddle, Tom. Good. Put your right foot in the other stirrup." She adjusted the length of the stirrup leather on both sides to accommodate Tom's length of leg. She *"click, click"*-ed to Nokto who sidled over so Lizzy could mount. (Tom thought Lizzy was beautiful as she mounted.) "Tom, see that thing sticking up on the front of the saddle. That's the horn. We use all Australian saddles here at Yellowood Farm. Grab hold of the horn if you need steadying. I'll control Two Sock's reins."

Accompanied by the two Jack Russell terriers, Lizzy and Tom rode out into bright sunlight. On the southern side of the barn, the flat land of Yellowood Farm was all green fields stitched with white, wooden, railed fences, dotted with horses grazing the succulent, emerald grass, and cows resting in other fenced-off portions. Lizzy, on Nokto, led them down a wide dirt path between fences. She pulled Tom on Two Socks up beside Nokto. "Now we can talk some more," she said.

"So. Who's in charge?" Tom asked, sitting straight in the saddle and looking around at the green, flat landscape.

"Uh? Of what?"

"Who's in charge of your farm?"

"Oh, well . . . Dillon's in charge of water use and reclamation, and maybe you could say Sheldon's in charge of horses . . . But nobody's *In Charge* of the farm. We all are, together."

"I mean, who makes important decisions?"

"We all do. But we rotate the job of facilitator. Nobody likes long meetings. We avoid'm when we can."

"Uh huh. Surely someone has the final say, when necessary."

"Bob-&-Dillon are the Seniors. They've been at Yellowood the longest, except for Jameka, who's retired. But we all — the adults, and sometimes the kids too — we all have to agree bout important things, like whether to add another animal to our responsibilities, or what strain of what vegetables to grow. Mostly we do what our experts recommend. Bob-&-Dillon, Torrin, and Jill, get their way too, I guess, lots of the time — since Kirsten-&-Jameka retired — because they have more experience, but we all try to keep them on their toes, and of course nothing happens til we all agree."

"Wow! Sounds like total anarkhy to me."

"Exactly. We're free. No bosses, no '*god damned government*' — as our ancestors often said — and absolutely no hierarchy."

"How can you get anything done without organization?"

"Oh, we're organized. Plenty. The whole Earth is organized. Just *not* at the point of a gun." Thumb cocked, Lizzy pantomimed shooting herself in the head with her index finger.

"Wait a minute. Who has the guns?" he asked.

"We have no guns. They were all melted down and salvaged for their metal fifteen hundred years ago, I think, when the few survivors were revolted by all the killing of the Final War."

"You always need guns for protection."

"We're not enemies. All of us. Ain't surrounded by enemies, as it seems people used to believe in the Elite Ages, before the Final War. Now, we're surrounded by family and friends, and potential friends, and other folks human like ourselves, in Solidarity. We've conquered xenophobia in ourselves, also long ago. We do not fear difference. We are, all of us, the Free People of Earth — [*Liberaj Homoj de la Tero*], in *Esperanto*—no matter who we are, who our myriad ancestors were, and where on the Earth they were from. Whether or not we are farmers, or anything else. We're all equal humans. We use gunpowder, as did the ancient Chinese, for fireworks celebrations, on Cinco de Mayo, for instance."

"Ah, oh, well . . . all that seems strange to me," Tom said. "But . . . what about your space program? Some sort of non-farmers, spacers, put up your satellites, yes?"

"Sure, but they live on Earth, on the remains of the Florida Peninsula, in Tavares Village, Lake-Florida County, within that circle of EnergyScreen-reinforced dikes, and have families who Farm. They all grew up on Farms, like everybody does. So they ain't alien. They're just folks like us who work in space sometimes."

"But, uh . . . Who co-ordinates it all? Don't you have any central control? For planetary projects, for instance?"

"Along with periodic local, regional, and continental meetings held more often, once every other decade we have a planetary meeting, where people from all over the planet meet in person to bond and discuss possible solutions to worldwide problems or proposed projects. It gives those who want-to a chance to travel.

"The last one was in 3675, eight years ago, held in Ulaanbaatar City, in Asia, once the capital of Mongolia and the only medium or large city on Earth not nuked during the Final War. It was almost empty then. . . . Mongolia had been devastated by the terrible social conditions on Earth at that time, and the climate was harsh and unpredictable. Were no jobs people in Ulaanbaatar could do for the rest of the world, to make the money necessary for life at that time in history, under the Elites and their Capitalism.

"End of the twenty-first century, fifty years or so before the Final War," Lizzy continued, "Ulaanbaatar had a population of over two million. At our last Census, in 3670, only bout six hundred thousand. Seemed like a lot of people to me. Less than six hundred thousand people in all of Lane County . . . People of Ulaanbaatar collectively Farm all the steppe round the city — under lots of domed EnergyScreens — south to the Gobi Desert.

"I went to that GlobalMeeting in 3675," she said, "on my YouthTrip. "Ulaanbaatar is a beautiful city, with lots of well-watered parkland, many museums, great exhibits of locally excavated dinosaur bones, and the popular campus of Ulaanbaatar Global University. The people there are very proud of their ancient city — the only non-radioactive city left on Earth — but they say most of the world's cities maybe weren't so very nice. . . .

"They were great hosts, although I was disappointed I didn't get to see the Gobi Desert — a great wilderness-preserve — because it was too far away from the city, and I had so many meetings I wanted to attend."

"What was the population of Earth," Tom asked, "before the, uh . . . Final War, and what is it now, do you know?"

"We have a planet-wide Census five years before every global meeting, done by the EarthCensus Syndic, and their periodic volunteer Workers. The last one was in 3670, thirteen years ago. bout nine hundred and thirty two million then, if I remember correctly. Might be one billion by the next census."

"Wow! Much lower than it was fifteen hundred years ago. How'd that happen?"

"From a population of over eighteen billion — mostly urban — in the mid-twenty-second century, just before the Final War, nuclear bombing of all the world's large and medium sized cities, with their suburbs, by both sides of the conflict, reduced the population of our planet to maybe a little more than two hundred million after the Elites abandoned us, leaving only rural people and wilderness dwellers behind on Earth. So, two hundred million people worldwide were what our ancestors collectively had to work with as they struggled to feed everyone, to build Solidarity among all the humans on Earth, to save the planet and its resources for their descendents, that is, for us."

Tom asked, "Why didn't the few people left after the Catastrophe of the Final War devolve into chaos and savagery? We've always known that savagery lurks beneath the surface of every human, despite the masquerade of so called '*civilization*'."

"Oh, Tom, *no! No!* That's what people in the Elite Ages were always taught to believe. That is, that all of *us*, the common, non-Elite people, are inherently cruel barbarians, vicious animals held back from destructive mob violence only by the civilizing effect of Elite leadership, organized religions, governments, and armed so-called 'guardians' among us. That we are — as ordinary, non-special, non-Elite human beings — inherently stupid, barely controlled beasts. But, actually, we're *not*," she hissed. "*Civilization is not a masquerade!*" Obviously, she was heated about the topic.

Lizzy continued: "We have reports from clear eyed observers—like Rebecca Solnit, in her great book, *A Paradise Built in Hell*, written more than sixteen centuries ago, in the very early twenty-first century on this continent, that — if elitist government and armed bullies would only leave them alone — ordinary people will, in terrible emergencies, band together in Solidarity and form communities of MutualAide to help each other survive. [**True!** ~ **Ed.**]

"That is, ordinary people who ain't elite or special in any way are always — might say instinctively — fine decent folks with a great capacity for neighborliness and the innate social skills to cooperate with others, in Solidarity, without government interference. Ordinary people can and will create civilization and voluntarily organize each other and their resources, to take care of everybody. In groups.

"Except in fascist societies, or in War, violent atrocities are usually performed by individuals alienated from their community," Lizzy concluded. "Humans are a social species, and failure of socialization was responsible for most individual violence in past times during the Elite Ages, we think today."

"Woo. I'll have to think about that," Tom said. "Umm, what were the two sides in the, uh, Final War?"

"Who knows? One bunch of economic tyrants using its national or corporate population as cannon fodder against another bunch of economic tyrants. We've learned since — there was never any reason for ordinary people to fight if only they had been allowed to control their own local resources and share with each other. When you share, it makes more for everybody. There's a Christian myth bout that, called 'The Loaves and the Fishes'. You know of it?"

"Yes. But not with that interpretation," Tom said.

"What interpretation you know?"

"It supposedly shows the power of God that Jesus had, to move people to do good deeds."

"So you're not a Christian?"

"I'm a nonbeliever," Tom said.

"You don't believe in God?"

"On Faraday, there is only one religion, Pauline-Christianity. If you're not a Christian, you're a non-believer. But I've always been a bit of an intellectual rebel, and I think I believe in God, just not in Faraday's version of the Christian God."

"Tell me bout that version. As an Anthropologist — though I don't have a *high* degree — I'm interested in all human religions and their influence on culture. I'd rather farm, and study independently, than spend years at a university," she explained.

"Well, according to a book written by my best friend, Bill McClevy, a professor of Earth-History," Tom said, "the Gospel story of Christianity changed on Faraday to include the story and travels of Saint Paul of Tarsus, who wrote most of what we call the New Testament. Pauline-Christianity believes that Paul was also an incarnation of the Son of God, the same Messiah, who deliberately disappeared after he was crucified, after his resurrection. He changed his name, avoided all His early disciples, and traveled the Earth to spread His Word Himself. Then, supposedly, He was beheaded in Rome when He was an old man, but He actually escaped and continued to travel throughout the world. An immortal, known as the Wandering Jew, He lived on into the twenty-second century after His crucifixion and founded His True Church — the First Jewish Church of Jesus Paul — among the best people, the Elites, which finally came to light on Faraday. Bill took a lot of heat — fortunately he survived it — for his opinions in that book of his, *Jesus Broken in Two*, and I learned a lot reading it. Monolithic religion always has to pretend there was never another form of that religion, never differing opinions, or people predisposed to think for themselves will be encouraged to disagree. So . . . Lizzy, do you consider yourself to be some sort of Christian?"

"No. I've always been some sort of *un*-affiliated Theist, like a lot of people here on Yellowood Farm, including Sheldon who is not a very religious Jew, just ethnically Jewish . . .'"

"Then religiously," Tom said, "even though I was born to the intellectually ridiculous religion of Faraday, I would fit right in at Yellowood Farm."

"Maybe so," she said, giving him an appraising look. Actually, she thought that — despite his abnormally pale skin, and his total lack of the skills needed to live and function as a farmer — he was rather an attractive, and interesting, man.

12

▼

THE INVADERS

Tom's friend Bill McClevy was a member of a Faradayan secret society, the Final Clones.

At the start, when Faraday was first settled, the original colonists — due to protein incompatibility with the alien environment — had been immune to all the diseases indigenous to their adopted planet. Which was fortunate, since the first few generations on Faraday were ones of unrelenting, backbreaking toil by the Working Class, harshly supervised by the leisured Elite. Disease among the actual, productive Workers would have ruined the colony.

Then, after five hundred years of growing Earth-crops in Faradayan soil, and breathing Faradayan air, the descendents of the Originals — both The Workers and the Elites — gradually became bio-chemically similar enough to the indigenous life forms of Faraday that they became susceptible to its diseases.

Beginning with the 25th generation after Landing, most humans were unexpectedly infected with a native *virus or prion*, which *severely aggravated their inherent, long-time, human tendency to xenophobia (fear of strangers)*.

Incidents of violence — especially toward the minority of people whose skin colour was non-'white' — had gradually increased in the colony. The phenomena had gone unnoticed at first, because violence as an expression of masculinity was considered normal, and the culture — Racist to begin with — still obsequious to the Elites, had no respect for non-violence in relation to diversity, nor did they have a social philosophy of peace. ("Namby pamby, wimpy *peace* is for cowardly *losers!*")

By the 29th generation, it had become obvious that xenophobia had increased in the population such that people of colour were becoming extinct on Faraday (something which did not bother most of the white majority), and then — after the *Fear-of-Strangers Disease* among the white population had eliminated nearly all of the *'Darkies'* — xenophobia had raged on, and misogyny had increased, driving men to kill their wives, sisters, daughters, or mothers because women were *alien*, inferior, *not men*. Then, when there were no more women, cloning became the only method possible of *'reproduction.'*

Descendents of the original Elites — subsequent generations of affluent men for several hundred years — cryo-froze clones generations ahead, until the practice became common on Faraday among the privileged. Some families were thus able to survive the millennia until the *Final Clones* secret society—founded by the 'great-great-grandson' of Bill's original Progenitor—had manipulated the government into sending probes to Earth to see if women still existed there. (Other planets settled by the Elites had women, of course, but their societies, like Faraday's, were militaristic, and it would not have been safe to approach them. Earth was presumed to be an easy, weak target.)

Unfortunately, when the probes had returned, bringing news that humans still lived on Earth, the Faradayan military had decided the presence of original humans on Earth was military intelligence of prime importance in their ongoing struggle for mastery of that part of the galaxy against other human colonies on other planets within a fifty-light-year radius of Earth.

'Struggle' meant *violence* to the military mind. Sending an expedition to Earth to *ask* for women—as if earth-women were the property of earth-men—was a wimpy, cowardly idea. To the military mind, **effective violence was the only way to solve problems**. Anyone not a real, patriotic Faradayan (white and male) was the enemy, and must be conquered. *Essential resources must be taken by force!*

The *Final Clones* secret society was made up of Faradayan men who had educated themselves over many generations, and had thus, they believed, culturally evolved into better men, progressive men suited to a more rational, sustainable, co-operative future. They had been frustrated and appalled when the military took over their idea to import women from Earth to solve Faraday's reproductive crisis. Thus Final Clones had infiltrated the military hierarchy of the expedition, adding to the number of their members who had already been drafted by the Military Invasion force.

When Bill McClevy heard his best friend Tom — not a Final Clone! — had been charged with Treason for returning a woman to Earth, Bill rejoiced. It meant his friend was a decent human being! Not a blind, **unthinking** xenophobe!

▼

The Moderator of the Colonels' group was Davidson, a Final Clone. He had skillfully convinced the Colonels to give up ravishing random countrysides. Destroying the infrastructure of the Earth was not part of their mission, he believed. The society of Faraday did not have to kill all the Earthers in order to survive. And slaughtering farmers was obviously a waste of ammunition.

However, he was unable to prevent the Colonels' Emergency Tactical Group from transferring the marauding Missouri forces immediately west of Kansas City. From there, they began a '*Sherman's March*' further westward, ravaging the countryside as they went, toward the area where ground surveillance had observed that the Traitor's stolen space-plane had touched down, returning a captured woman to Earth.

13

▼

PEASANT-EARTH

Near the sprawl of semi-wild woodland which separated Yellowood Farm from the next farm to the south — Apiary-Blossom Farm, which supplied honey to all of Lane County — with Lizzy controlling Two Socks' reins, she and Tom were out riding at the far southern edge of Yellowood's furthest pasture, when Lizzy's eTabb rang in her pocket. She took it out.

"What?" she asked.

"Lizzy, our robocams have spotted the Invaders coming our way!" Dillon's voice shouted from the eTabb. "We have to raise the Shield. Get home now!"

"Come on!" Lizzy shouted, slapping Two Socks on the rump. "Tom! Grab hold of the horn! Hang on!"

Tom clutched the horn on his saddle, fighting to stay upright. He was terrified he would fall off as *Two Socks* followed close on Nokto's back end. He could see nothing but Lizzy riding expertly ahead of him, and his horse's front shoulders working hard beneath its foaming pelt. Yapping, the two Jack Russell terriers led the rush.

The pounding, rough, barbaric ride didn't, to his shock, end at the cob barn, but rather beyond it, at several canopies pitched on the K-96 highway past the earth-berm of the Yellowood Earthship®.

▼

Lizzy was showing Tom how to slowly walk the horses around to help them cool down when the Shield went up with a soft crackle — eliciting a great chorus of dog barking — over both Yellowood and Rosebud Earthships®, not including either farm's out-buildings, (their animal residents had all been moved to the canopies). The too-small Shield also had left all of Yellowood's pasturage vulnerable along with Rosebud's grain fields.

After Lizzy rubbed down and brushed the horses — Tom watching intently as she explained how to check for possible sores and other problems with the horses' hides — they walked back under the dome of the Farm-Shield to the Yellowood Earthship®. Lizzy showed him around the inside of the residence, explaining how the Earthship® actually worked to keep them cool in the summer and warm in the winter.

"Now," she said, waving her arms to illustrate her words, "With the sun coming in, at an angle, through the sloped south glass of the greenhouse corridor for twelve to sixteen hours a day in the late spring, summer, and early fall, with the sun high in the sky, it heats up the greenhouse real good. So we use opaque sunshield blinds over the *stay*glass of the GatherRoom's south wall and in our bedrooms, to keep that intense heat out the inside-rooms. Ventilation tubes in all the rooms' solid backwalls are kept open when it's hot outside. We screen them, keeping small animals and insects out. Air coming in is cooled by traveling through the earth of the berm.

"Feel that," she said, putting her hand in front of the nearest ventilation tube's opening. "Cooler than the room's ambient temperature. Then we open the skylights of the dormers outside each room, over the greenhouse, with these nice ropes right here, and the unwanted warm air goes up and out — through the open transoms over each door and each tall glass window — pulling more cool air in from the ventilation tubes."

Motioning him to sit down with her in two easy chairs set apart from the area where several Yellowood communards were intently watching the 2D feed from robocams monitoring the Invaders in their area, she continued her lecture: "In winter, the sun is lower in the sky and the sunlight comes in at right angles through the sloped windows and first heats up the greenhouse corridor. We eliminate the sunshield blinds so the sun's warmth can come right into our living spaces and it's stored in the high thermal mass of the thick side and back walls, and this big pillar here," she said, slapping it. "In winter, and really cold days in spring and autumn, we keep the skylights, the transoms, and the ventilation tubes closed — see there the little ventilation door we can close? — to keep out the cold air.

"Voila ! The earth and sun do it all — 'Mother Earth, Father Sun', as Indigenous American folklore teaches us — organic heating and cooling, eliminating the need for outside fuel."

"I'm impressed," Tom said. "Seems effortless."

"Physics does it all. Of course, we have to build the Earthships® correctly, so they work well. We've known how to do that for seventeen hundred years since the twentieth century when Michael Reynolds and his Green Disciples experimented with Earthship-Biotecture®. They struggled with the Elites so he could design and build homes like our Earthships®, where people didn't have to pay money for basics like heating, cooling, water, electricity, and vegetables."

"Vegetables? . . . Um, money. We should talk about money. Okay?" he asked.

"Sure . . ." She sat comfortably and waited. "Well?"

"I don't see how money fits into your culture."

"Doesn't"

"What?" he asked, confused.

"Don't use money," she said. "Don't *have* money."

"How? What? It's the basic medium of exchange!"

"Don't need money for exchange. We just share."

"But, well . . . What if some people take more than they need? How do you control that?"

"Groups who waste food and other materials would eventually not be shared with. Actually, their neighbors would have long before helped them solve that problem. Obviously, people who eat too much get sick, with damaged hearts or livers, or other diseases. Stuff other than food must be stored and handled by the individual, and too much stuff is a burden . . . I don't know. We've never seriously had the problem. But, in moneyed cultures, didn't some few individuals accumulate more money than most, and the social power went with it? And they defended their irresponsible, antisocial glut with violence? People with excessive amounts of money got to live in extreme luxury without doing any useful work. Didn't they—?"

"Here they come! Blasting Grasshopper Farm now!" shouted a communard watching the robo-cam telefeed on the 2D screen.

"Their Shield up?" Lizzy asked.

"Aye," someone answered.

Lizzy jumped up and ran through the greenhouse corridor out the south exit to the temporary wall of the FarmShield cutting across Yellowood's big garden. Tom and others followed her. They stood on the straw-strewn dirt path of the garden under the FarmShield and watched a mini tank approach. "Frack it!" Lizzy swore. "Our barn."

"We'll have to re-build it," Dillon said quietly behind her. "And we've got to enlarge and reconfigure our Partnership's Shield so it covers both our farms completely: gardens, fields, at the very least the outbuildings."

"Been lazy," Ora said bitterly, "putting it off cause no tornado has come our way in so long. Now know we have to do it."

Tom watched — surprised by his nausea and anger at the Invaders' casual use of violence against the People of Earth — as a mini-tank burned the fences and pasturage of Yellowood Farm, blew apart the cob barn — fortunately with no animals in it, not even chickens — and advanced to burn that part of the garden outside the Shield.

"Got all the eggplant!" someone behind Tom said angrily.

"Almost ready to pick," Lizzy sighed.

The mini tank ran its treads up against the wall of the FarmShield which fizzed in response. The man on top of the tank aimed its big gun at the people inside the Shield. Tom recognized Keith Richardson. "Sh-should we just stand here?" Tom asked Lizzy.

"Shield either protects us, or we're all dead," she said. "Ain't no matter where we stand."

The Sergeant fired steel shells at the Farm-Shield. The whole area of the Shield in front of them instantly became opaque, but it didn't break. Richardson aimed the flamethrower next. The Shield held. Not even the heat came through.

The mini tank backed suddenly away from the Shield, skewed backwards through the ruined garden and the debris of the cob barn outside the Shield, and quickly disappeared, presumably on its way to help decimate the out-of-Shield areas of either Pinklight or Rosebud Farms.

The communards and their visitor trooped back inside the Earthship®, relieved the Farm-Shield had protected them, depressed the attack had happened at all.

"Now we're in a state of siege," Bob Beiler told them. "Be no more water, no matter how much it rains, until we're safe to turn off the Shield. We *do* have the bathtubs we filled a few days ago."

"Come on, Folks.," Dillon Ness added. "Out of yall's slumps. Have a siege to survive. Remember to *not* flush the toilets very often."

"Uh, stinky," someone said.

▼

Lizzy and her communards settled down quickly after the attack and began to prepare supper together. Some stacked dishes and flatware on one end of their kitchen prep table, for buffet style serving. Others wielded knives, slicing plantains on the diagonal, cutting tomatoes into thin half circles, and dicing mushrooms. Tom saw the woman he identified as 'white' — Bekky Shields — quietly frying the plantain slices and the mushroom pieces, while tending pots of whole-grain rice and black beans on the electric stove. Lizzy explained to Tom the stove was powered by the Earthship®'s batteries supplied by photo-voltaic panels and three windmills on the roof. "Now, under the Shield, will have just the solar panels," she said.

The men and women shared equally in the work. Even the Farm's children were able to help. Tom was parked at the big dining table, 'out of the way', because they hadn't time to show him what to do.

▼

Tom was surprised at how delicious the supper was, totally vegetarian, no meat at all. "Most farmers can't bear to kill and eat our own animal friends," Lizzy clarified, salting her plantain slices. "But some people are able to butcher sheep, cattle, pigs, llamas, chickens, turkeys, ducks, goats, or rabbits that die of natural causes, genetically programmed to go off in the animals' old ages. I admit, the animals we can eat were bred over the last fifteen hundred years to live long healthy lives and drop dead, painlessly, of brainstem aneurysms, so those of us who like meat — and I admit I'm one — don't have to face killing our animal friends in their prime," she said, squeezing a lime to drizzle juice over her plantain slices. "When they die, we give the bodies of our animals to Butcher Farm a few miles south of us, and the butchers there prepare and tenderize the meat for everyone in Lane County. Still, since we have no meat industry as such on this planet, we don't eat meat at every meal. Neither do the butchers."

"Sounds like a very humane way of doing things," Tom said.

"Some people—like our county Vet, Nan Diller, who's totally vegetarian—think it's morally wrong to bioengineer animals to die of aneurysms just to feed the few of us who want to eat meat. She says we have, as the human species, long known how to get complete protein from plants and we ought to do that. We remind her that in an earlier age, if she wanted to be morally correct, she would have had to be a vegan and not eat milk, butter, cheese, or eggs produced by animals exploited terribly. But since we can now produce enough fresh, local milk for everyone in each county on this planet and we don't overwork our dairy cows' nor our goats' udders, or kill and eat as veal the non-milk-producing young male animals born, we ain't abusing any animals to overproduce, for profit—for *money*—milk and other dairy foods. We limit the number of male cattle born, to facilitate natural reproduction, then let them live their lives, free in our fields. Also, we don't keep hens in cages their entire lives to lay eggs for us and then eat the chickens when the entire coop decreases its laying production, but instead we let them roam the barnyard and live a more natural life, until they die of brainstem aneurysms. So *vegan*ism is not morally necessary. At least some of us carnivore-types think."

"Well, I know that beans and brown rice are a complete protein, and I'm glad to have some cheese with it," Tom said, grinning at Lizzy, feeling, at that moment, comfortable in his exile.

"Mango slices for dessert," Sheldon said. "And we have coffee — from freshly picked beans— from Pinklight, to keep us awake at our farm-meet."

14

▼

PEASANT-EARTH

They started right after supper, seated around the dining table, after everyone — including Tom, who was glad there was something he could help with — had cleared the table. The communards lay their eTabbs face up in front of them, ready to take notes, if necessary. Tom's expensive Faradayan phone was useless for anything other than talking.

Tom was surprised to find a purring calico cat on his lap. Fortunately, his long-ago ancestors had taken fertile cats with them when they left Earth. Tom was familiar with the species. He had *'owned'* a cat on Faraday, so he knew how to respond to the flattery of having a cat sit on his lap. He petted her softly, feeling sad about his long-dead cat, *'Dinger'* (short for Schrodinger). He was still angry and heartsick that the military had forced him to abandon the cat when he was drafted.

"The cat's name is Cleo," Lizzy whispered. "she's a special friend of mine."

The farm-meet, facilitated by Jill's egg-daughter, eleven year old, copper-coloured Bozena Dighton — *apparently as practice in basic social skills* — began first with a brief story by Manda, explaining the horror of what had happened to Suzie and how she herself had come to return to Yellowood Farm so quickly. She had begun speaking in *Esperanto*, as *la Homoj de la Tero* [the People of Earth] always did at residence meetings, to keep in practice for larger meetings with people who did not speak their ethnic language. Tom was obviously excluded from understanding.

Frowning, Lizzy suggested they speak Ameriglish for the rest of that evening's meet, so they could include Tom who had brought Manda back to them.

Then the communards quizzed Tom — with faint hostility, despite their gratitude for his having rescued Manda at the cost of exiling himself — asking him to tell them about the Invaders and what they wanted.

He explained about clones and Faraday's reproduction crisis. His understated agitation disturbed the cat who jumped off his lap.

"What! Yall killed all yall's women a thousand years ago?" Sheldon shouted.

"Yall think we're just walking wombs?" Marsha asked, nastily.

"I would rather not reproduce than use your sperm!" Jill shouted, red-faced.

"Disgusting!"

"Barbarians!"

"Suzie was 'too dark'? What! What? Yall filthy—"

Despite her own emotional turmoil, Bozena said — rising to her duty as Facilitator — "All right, *all right!* Does anyone else have a . . . um . . . calm . . ?"

She looked down at her mother for help. Since at her age she had not yet begun to spurt up in height, she was standing on her chair.

"Restrained," Jill suggested.

". . . uh, a restrained comment to give Tom bout the Invaders?" Bozena finished.

Brown-skinned Aisha McHenry stuttered, furious, "Yall . . . yall — aliens — come to Earth, eh? . . . and . . . and . . . destroy our loved ones, our farmland, our animals, our neighbors, be . . . be, be, because—"

"Because!" George W.C. Healy raised his voice, "Yall were stupid and killed women!"

"Frack it!" Lizzy shouted. "Let's all calm down and let Bozena center the meeting!"

"Aye," Jill said, looking abashed. "Let's show some respect for Bozena and the process. Sorry, sweetheart," she said to her daughter. "You know how Yellowood folk are always so opinionated and hot headed."

"Okay, people, shipmates. Let's go on," Bozena said softly. She sat down.

D'mitri Dauphin spoke up, quietly, saying to Tom: "Women of Earth ain't *things* for yall outer-space men to steal away from us, eh? They are people —"

"Aye, people," Bekky Shields said. "And —"

"Please, Bekky," Bozena pleaded, "let's not interrupt."

"Sorry," Bekky said. "Go on, D'mitri."

"Tom," D'mitri said, taking hold of Tom's hand — a gesture which embarrassed the Faradayan greatly — "How can we negotiate a peace settlement with your former comrades? That's the important issue here, I think. Right?" he asked his shipmates. They all nodded, hands covering their mouths.

"Peace settlement . . . uh," Tom answered, gently pulling his hand away from D'mitri. "That's the problem. The Faradayan military did not expect to *fail* at invading Earth and taking, umm, the women."

"Female *things*," Bekky sneered.

"Go on," Bozena said, leaning close over the table, vibrating with concern, almost standing again on her chair.

"The problem is," Tom continued, "the Faradayan expedition to Earth was originally conceived as a civilian endeavor, but then the military took it over. The Generals and the Colonels are not inclined to negotiate. Winning, beating the enemy completely, is the only outcome they can accept. They are not rational, reasonable, or even sane on the subject."

"*Frack*," Lizzy swore. "Profiteering scumbags," Sheldon snarled at the same time.

"Shipmates . . ." Bozena quickly warned.

"So what can we do?" D'mitri asked Tom.

Tom rubbed his blonde head, thinking. "Let me see if I can contact a friend of mine in the Faradayan Army. Bill McClevy. He belongs to a secret anti-military group — didn't save him from being drafted — but maybe he, and others of his group, can help." Tom sat back in his chair and picked up his personal phone.

The meeting continued, in **Esperanto**. Tom quietly asked Lizzy why. She told him they had switched to discussing farm business. "Right now, we're talking bout the need to rebuild the cob barn."

"Lizzy, *kaj vi?*" ["how bout you?"] Bob Beiler asked.

"Jes, kompreneble." ["Aye, of course."], Lizzy answered. "Tom, I need to take part in this conversation. I haven't time to translate. Why don't you call your friend on the starship now?"

"Okay."

15

▼

THE INVADERS

Bill McClevy had been wounded on the surface of the Shield over Kansas City. The ricochet, hitting him in the side, had opened him up and nicked his liver. Having lost a great deal of blood, he was recovering in the Medical Bay of the starship parked behind the Moon at Lagrange Point **L2**. The medics had sewed-up his damaged liver.

Bill was restless. As a Final Clone, he felt a responsibility to break the military's intractable hold on the impossible situation with the Earthers, so they could move forward and negotiate for women or eggs to solve Faraday's acute reproduction problem.

Shortly before they were drafted, since he and Tom Worthington were friends — and in an effort to recruit him as a new member of the Final Clones — Bill had given Tom a personal phone and his private number. He had explained that he belonged to a secret lodge consisting of men who were sworn to help each other live well in the highly competitive, Capitalist society on Faraday.

Private, personal phones were extremely expensive — lest common men easily communicate with each other, disrupting the elitist status quo. In the Army, Bill's phone, since it was a privilege to own one, was part of his *personal* kit, which the Faradayan military allowed men, *as part of their honor,* to keep apart from the periodic, official inspections of their Sergeants.

Bill's phone rang, and he hastily answered it. The radio signals of the phone were scrambled at the source and unscrambled only at the receiver, so their conversations were always private.

"Bill? You there?"

"Yes. Tom is it?"

"Yes. Listen, I've gotten to know the Earthers recently, and I believe they won't surrender under any circumstances. Can your lodge-brothers help with that? With the Colonels?"

"I don't think so. Only one of us is a Colonel. You know how they are. Are there any concessions the Earthers will accept? Maybe a base with 100,000 soldiers — and the surveillance satellites left behind — to protect them from the rest of the Galaxy?"

"I think they'd feel they would need protection from the Faradayan soldiers. They are very angry about *Every. Single. Earther.* who's been killed so far. No matter what age, colour, or sex. And they wouldn't want to provide food to a group of armed men who, in their opinion, would make no positive contribution to their society."

"So you've gotten to know those Earthers pretty well, eh?"

"Ah . . . yes." Tom knew what Bill meant: Sex. He wished Bill's guess was correct —

"Okay! Listen," Bill said. "I'll see what we can do here, as soon as they let me out of Sickbay."

"Great. Thanks, Bill." I'll let the Earthers know at their next meeting."

▼

Unfortunately, although the military could not unscramble the words in the signals between two private phones, nevertheless the actual exchange of radio waves had been noted, pinpointing the location of both ends of the conversation.

As soon as Bill hung up his phone, a small squad of soldiers entered his sickroom and the squad's Sergeant arrested him for Treason for secretly communicating with the Traitor on Earth. They yanked him out of bed, pulling the IVs from his arms, and severed his connections to the monitoring machines.

He was quickly taken to the brig, chained to a bed, and left alone.

▼

Once again, the Colonels met in the "War Room" of the starship. "Those god-damned Earther cowards are invulnerable!"

Before the rest of the Colonels could express the fury he could see blazing from all of them, Davidson — the Moderator, secretly a Final Clone — said, "We could spend lots of time, men, and materials destroying the infrastructure of the Earth. We could eventually conquer them. But there might not be any living people left. We must remember that *women* are the goal. We need women, for sexual reproduction, for genetic mixing."

"They must give us eggs, thousands of white eggs, . . white eggs," the oldest Colonel snapped.

"We het-men want the women for sex," the youngest Colonel snarled.

"We need women who are not too bright," said the colonel who questioned everything. "Smart women tend to think they're people. No end of trouble. So my family history passed down from the Originals tells me. Women not too goddamned bright."

"With eggs, we can grow our own women, give them no education. Walking wombs, barely smart enough to wipe themselves," added the Colonel who was interested only in objective truth.

"Vaginas," snarled the youngest Colonel, expressing his sexual frustration.

"Gentlemen!" Moderator Davidson said, "we need to spend our time discussing how to get the women! Everything else is details we can settle later."

"What we need to do," said the next to the oldest Colonel, "is *nuke* that shitty land outside the EnergyScreens. The Screens they stole from us. Protecting *mud* farmhouses, for Paul's Sake!" He paused to catch his breath and wipe the froth of fury from his lips. Some small spittle ran down his chin. Impatiently, he rubbed it off. "Then, when they realize they have only their houses under the EnergyScreens, with no food or water, or good air, and the land all around them is radioactive, we offer to rescue them all, if they surrender and leave the Domes. Then we can kill all their cowardly males, and all the Darkies, and capture the

white women and take them back to Faraday. Mission accomplished."
He looked around — smug — and glared at all the other Colonels.

"Yes, get the women."

"Nuke the whole damned planet."

"God-damned Earthers, playing Dog-in-the-Manger with their women."

"Fuck'em. Fuck'em all!"

"Death to the Earthers! The women are *ours!*"

The Moderator got up and quickly left the room.

Moments later, heavily armed and armored soldiers, all Final Clones, burst in the main doors and began firing at the Colonels, intending to slaughter them all. The doomed officers had no chance to use their pistols.

The room was full of flying, ricocheting lead for less than a minute.

One Colonel's corpse, trapped upright in its chair between the table and a pile of dead bodies behind, gradually became headless as one soldier concentrated all his firepower on its head, splattering pieces of brain, bone and gore all around, venting his rage as a rape victim of the mostly heterosexual Colonel who had become besotted with the soldier's small stature and (so-called) *'feminine'* features.

The exultant rape victim screamed in triumph as the firing stopped when all the Colonels were obviously dead.

▼

Bill was crusty with blood from where the IVs had been yanked from his arms. A backless med gown was the only clothing the jail guards had allowed *the god-damned-Traitor*, Corporal William McClevy. He lay shackled to the bed in a cell for several days—an eternity of boredom and pain for him, with intermittent food and water, and very little of that—waiting for the court-martial leading inevitably to his execution. He was in deep despair, worrying about himself as well as Tom and the rescue mission the military had usurped from the secret Lodge the 'g'g'grandson' of his Progenitor had founded.

He was released by a group of Final Clones, draftees all, who told him about The Slaughter of the Colonels by the Final Clones.

"We knew they would be arrogant and stupid and destroy the entire planet if the Earthers didn't surrender," Arnold Bates, a tall red-headed Private, told Bill, "and that would not get us the women we need to save Faraday."

"Please understand I am grateful to be out of that damned cell," Bill said. "But killing every Colonel except Davidson — you *did* spare Davidson, I hope; he's one of us — It reinforces the stupid, old, xenophobic notion that '*killing people is the best way to solve social problems*,' and that's not what the philosophy of our Lodge has come to be all about —"

"When they arrested you —"

"Did you spare Davidson?" Bill asked, irritated.

"Yes, of course, but —"

"But what?"

"We were determined, we had all agreed, so he let us kill them as soon as he left the Hall, but he said he would *not* lead us. He said that you, Professor, should do it, because your family founded the Final Clones."

"Oh, hell. I'm not a military expert. I don't know tactics. I'm just an historian."

"So you know the Earthers better than anyone." Redheaded Bates looked stubborn.

"Damn . . . All right. Tell Davidson I'll do it if he serves as my chief advisor."

▼

A few minutes later, back in his own four-man quarters, in a comfortable uniform stripped of a Corporal's insignia, Bill was relieved when Davidson reported to him.

"Are you sure you can't take this job? I'm only a history professor," Bill said to the older man. "Fully out of my element here."

"You're one of the men. They respect you," Davidson answered. "You're one of us too."

"I argued much too strongly against slaughtering all the other Colonels. I'm lucky they didn't shoot me too."

"Damn your ass."

"Well, Bill. We all have our Cross to bear, sooner or later. But perks . . . each Colonel had his own private quarters. Pick the one you want, . . . um, other than mine. I'll have a couple of the men clear it out and move your things."

"Damn. All right. Have my — now — former roommates do it. They'll know what's my stuff. And have them save all the liquor. We're gonna need it. I know the Colonels had a lot of good booze."

"I'll text the Generals back on Faraday to ask tactical advice."

"They won't help," Bill snarled.

▼

Bill was right. When Davison used the ansible and asked for advice, (omitting the slaughter of all the other Colonels), the Generals replied:

▼

SUCCESS ESSENTIAL – EARTH MUST YIELD – GET THE WOMEN FAILURE MEANS DEATH

▼

"I'm not sure whose death they mean: us soldiers or our civilization on Faraday," Davidson told Bill.

"Or the Earth itself . . . Well, we're on the scene. The Generals can't touch us," Bill said. "First we have to get the women, without destroying the Earth. Our natal planet, for Paul's sake. Then we'll figure out how to save ourselves."

"The arrogance! The hubris!" Davidson growled. "To make such a thuggish threat when they can't really back it up! And thinking we'll be frightened and obey! So much is at stake! When reasonable compromise could guarantee a future for Faraday, they are more concerned with their need to win, to decimate the enemy! — Earthers are the enemy because they have what we want and they're descended from 'Losers!'— Bah!"

"With their defenses, the only way we can fulfill our mission is to negotiate with the Earthers as equals. They have us by the short-hairs now," Bill sighed.

"You said you wanted my advice," Davison said. "Call your friend the Traitor on Earth."

▼

"Tom. Here's our offer," Bill spoke into his phone. "We'll leave Earth alone forever if 100,000 white women — or their ovaries in cryofreeze — come back to Faraday with us."

"The people here at this Farm are joining an ongoing worldwide electronic meeting tomorrow. I'll communicate your suggestion," Tom said.

16

▼

PEASANT-EARTH

After the farm-meeting, Lizzy said to Tom, "Why don't you bunk in my room tonight?"

"Oh, don't you have a guest room?" *What's the matter with me?* Tom thought. *She can't mean to <u>sleep</u> only!*

"This Earthship® isn't an elitist, lah-dee-dah mansion," Lizzy snarled. "We have no '*guest rooms*'. Sleep on the GatherRoom floor for all I care!" She stomped out into the greenhouse corridor and disappeared into the thick greenery.

Tom stood stunned, sick with his own stupidity.

"Tom," Bob Beiler said quietly behind him.

Tom turned and faced the bearded older man. "What?" His ears were ringing.

"Out that door." Bob pointed. "Turn right into the greenhouse and her room is the third door off the corridor, on your right. Go on now. Yall het-men need to be tougher, wanting women as you do."

"She's angry," Tom said, gulping his unease.

"So what? She's my shipmate. I know her. She's totally heterosexual and she hasn't had a man in a long time. You're in luck. Go on."

"You sure?"

"Aye. Aye. Go on now, or be fracked, frack it, Tom."

▼

Tom went out into the corridor, thick with greenery, and found Lizzy's door easily. He knocked gently and said softly, "Lizzy, it's Tom. Can I sleep in your bed tonight?"

She jerked the door open. She was naked. A real woman. And beautiful! No robot had *ever* looked that good. He forgot to breathe. Her belly was flat, her legs long and strong. She looked soft all over, but not hairless. She was covered with a dark reddish-golden fuzz on her arms and legs and the magic place between her thighs. Her breasts stood up proudly.

"Come to bed then," Lizzy said.

He flowed into her welcoming arms knowing he had been waiting for her all his life.

▼

"Why are you still soft, Tom? Don't you find me attractive?"

"Oh, no, I . . . I mean, that's not it. I just never . . ."

"So. You've never had sex with a real woman before. Have you?"

"No, uh . . . I —"

"How delightful. I get to be your first. Don't worry. I like to be the prime mover sometimes." She touched him knowingly. Her *non-robot eyes* were alive with desire.

He shuddered with sudden pleasure, and felt his cock grow hard. *She actually wants me!* Since he was in the top position, he moved to enter her as he had a robot many times.

He could never remember exactly how she did it, but suddenly he was on his back. She was on top. With practiced hands, she positioned his erection, and with a quick downward thrust, she engulfed him. She leaned over and brushed the tips of her breasts through the hair on his chest. He shivered, trembled, and orgasmed immediately. *Her real woman's body is exquisite!*

She was obviously disappointed, and he realized dimly, as he fell blissfully asleep, that sex with a woman must also mean — as it never had with a robot — that she wanted pleasure too.

He soon woke to find her caressing him again. She kissed him. "Mmm, Tom-Tom, let's do that again. I want some fun too. Been a long time for me."

"Again, yes," he mumbled. "I'd like to stay connected longer, if, um, you don't mind." He caressed her beautiful breasts with both his hands. "Let's take it easy now," she gasped. "Mmm, you on top. . . ."

▼

The next morning, waked by soft melodious bells, Tom wanted to luxuriate in bed, but Lizzy was energetic, up and around, hurriedly dressing in what looked to his Faradayan eyes like 'men's clothes'.

"I've got barn work," she said. "You can sleep 'til second bells, and then you have to get up if you want breakfast. The eMeet starts at 8AM our time, right after breakfast." She kissed him on the mouth, opened her bedroom door into the greenhouse corridor, and left quickly.

He groaned with disappointment.

▼

Breakfast was scrambled eggs, crispy re-fried plantain slices left over from supper, shredded potatoes, fresh hibiscus petals, crunchy dried black currants, sliced melon, buttered toast, a glass of milk, and coffee or tea.

"One mug apiece, please," Dillon told everyone. "We must start conserving water now, at the beginning of the siege."

Bob explained to Tom (and the younger children) how the Electronic World-Meet would work: "During the Crisis of 2516, a small group of would-be-Elites tried to bring back representative democracy and ruin the freedom of our global Anarkhy so they — the would-be pseudo-Elites — could be in charge and be *privileged* thereby. They tried often, loudly and repeatedly, to convince everyone their ideas were in the vast majority. Many folks were almost convinced. . . .

"But com-experts from all over the world combined their talents, wrote great code, and developed programming whereby everyone could quickly know during an electronic meeting what we all actually agreed on, or how we disagreed, and where we were blocked from over 96% consensus."

"The software is brilliant," Ora Dighton added. "No one today, over a thousand years later, can imagine how we could ever make emergency worldwide decisions without the ***Interkonsento /Centra*** ['***Consensus /***

Central'] programming, as it's called. So we don't need the elitism and the potential dangers of laws and *representative* democracy."

"*Privilege*, for anyone, for any reason, is a bad idea," Jill added.

▼

"Has everyone got their tea or coffee and something maybe to munch on?" Bekky asked. "Okay, let's clear the table, and move to the 2D screen. Will need the large one. Ri—"

Tom interrupted. "Let me do it. I haven't been much help so far, and I *do* know how to clear table. Please?"

"No," Bekky said. "You have to participate at the beginning of the eMeet by telling all the people of Earth bout the Invaders, how they are, what might get them to depart Earth and leave us alone. Clearing the table goes fastest when we all help."

"Okay," Tom said reluctantly.

Lizzy slipped her arm around his waist. "You're starting to fit right in. That's good." She smiled fondly at him.

▼

Tom and the shipmates of Yellowood Earthship® sat in comfortable chairs in their GatherRoom—the dining table was cleared and pushed aside—in full view of the large 2D Screen. Anelia Dighton, their fifteen year old, tapped up the eMeet net-site: the screen displayed the info for the ElectronicMeeting (in *Esperanto*):

>>>>>>>>>>> ELEKTRONIKA KUNVENO, 8a SEPTEMBRO, 3683 <<<<<<<<<<<

▼

FROM 7ᵗʰ SEPTEMBER
PRELIMINARY CONSENSUS 99.98%

NO WOMAN ON EARTH WANTS TO EXILE HERSELF TO A PLANET OF MISOGYNOUS MEN

OR DONATE AN OVARY TO THE
CONTROL OF MISOGYNOUS MEN

▼

QUESTIONS SO FAR

WHAT IS A LIGHT YEAR?
WHY DOES EARTH NOT HAVE A
DEEP SPACE PROGRAM?
DO WE WANT TO EXPORT OUR
EGALITARIAN CULTURAL IDEALS
TO THE REST OF THE (HUMAN) GALAXY?
WHAT SHALL WE DEMAND AS RECOMPENSE
FOR OUR DEAD LOVED ONES?

▼

FURTHER DISCUSSION IN 286 SECONDS

▼

"Okay. You ready, Tom?
"Yes."
"Manda?"
"Aye."

▼

Tom's face appeared on the Screen as he explained, for everyone on Earth who had joined that eMeet — Lizzy beside him translating into *Esperanto* — the psychology of the Faradayan military, the reproduction crisis on Faraday and what caused it, and how he came to be a Traitor and an exile.

Where's the camera? Tom thought, glancing around. (The camera-lens was in millions of pieces, only a few atoms wide each, hiding among the pixels of the 2D screen.)

Tom told the people of Earth what he believed the price of peace needed to be, emphasizing Faraday's desperation.

Manda spoke next, in *Esperanto,* recounting the horror of what had happened to her twin, Susie, on their YouthTrip. As she began speaking, hoarse with grief and repressed fury, her haggard face appeared on the Screen. Tom's face disappeared when he fell silent.

Then the Screen was filled with more and more pictures getting smaller and smaller, millions of human faces speaking *Esperanto.* In their farm-residences, hostels, factories, or village halls, everyone-at-once was expressing to the world how they felt about what Tom or Manda had said. All the participants argued their own ideas about what to do with the Invaders and their siege of Earth.

The large 2D Screen sparkled as millions of tiny new faces continuously replaced the faces of those who had stopped speaking. The software recorded everyone who spoke, in case people needed to check and confirm what the programming concluded were the Agreements arrived at, and the eventual Consensus solving the problem. People rarely checked. Because it included automatically the input of every person who spoke:, the global-programming *Interkonsento /Centra* was universally trusted. It had always worked very well, to everyone's satisfaction, whatever global decision was ultimately reached.

No one on Earth in that year 3683 suggested pale-skinned women be *forced* to go to Faraday or even to give away their ovaries. Manda became very angry when one idea was suggested by enough individuals all over the world so the programming typed it on the screen:

▼

!!!!!!!!! LEGACY-EGGS FROM 100,000 LIGHT-
SKINNED, DEAD WOMEN !!!!!!!
!!!!!!!!!! BE GIVEN THE FARADAYANS TO MAKE THEM GO AWAY!!!!!!!!!

▼

In a global answer shouted at their screens by millions of people (women, men, trans-folk, and herms), the Yellowood 2D screen sparkled in a particularly ferocious way (in *Esperanto*):

▼

!!!!!!!!!!!! WE MUST NOT BREAK TRUST !!!!!!!!!!!!
!!!!!!!! WITH OUR ANCESTORS WHO GAVE
US THEIR LEGACY EGGS: !!!!!!!
!!!!!!!!!!!! LIKE ALL WOMEN ALIVE TODAY !!!!!!!!!!!!!
!!!!!!!! THEY WOULD <u>NOT</u> WISH MISOGYNY !!!!!!!!
!!!!!!!! ON THEIR UNBORN DAUGHTERS !!!!!!!!

▼

Then millions of BirthHouse Workers from everywhere on Earth spoke over and over, identifying their village, and their profession, and saying they would never break promises made to the dead who had, in Solidarity, donated their genetic material to future generations of the Anarkhy on Peasant-Earth. The women who had given their ovaries as Legacy-Eggs to their local BirthHouses had believed their unborn descendents would inherit the peaceful, egalitarian world they themselves had been part of and had contributed to all their lives.

Quickly, every single BirthHouse on Earth (by the numbers) pledged to *never* release *any* of their Legacy-Eggs for export to the misogynist planet Faraday. Or *any* planet other than Earth.

Manda Dighton, angry, red faced, marching about, waving her arms, fired up her shipmates to chant *"Neniu ofero! Neniu ofero!"* ("No sacrifice! No sacrifice!") and millions of people worldwide did the same. Soon it appeared, in *Esperanto*, on the screen:

▼

KONSENTON 98.6%

((CONSENSUS 98.6%))

▼

!!!!! NO SACRIFICE OF LEGACY EGGS !!!!!
!!!!! NO SACRIFICE OF LEGACY EGGS !!!! NO
SACRIFICE OF LEGACY EGGS !!!!!
!!!! NO SACRIFICE !!!!! NO SACRIFICE !!!!! NO
SACRIFICE !!!!! NO SACRIFICE !!!!

▼

Earth's unique global conversation — everyone talking at once, sorted by the *Interkonsento /Centra* programming — continued for many hours. The Yellowood shipmates took staggered breaks away from their sparkling screen to sit and talk around their kitchen prep table.

"I'm afraid if Earth decides not to help the Faradayans," Dillon said sadly, "the starship will nuke the planet, trapping us inside our Shields, and —"

"No! That must not happen!" Tom barked. "We'll run out of water, and food —"

"No, Tom. We can adjust the system and recycle water indefinitely. We can feed all of us, without much variety, it's true, from our greenhouse garden —"

"But air!" Tom said. "And the cloud-cover created by the nukes will block out the sunlight we need for electricity! The windmills can't help with no wind —"

"The Shields are great engineering," Ora told him. "They clean the air they let in. But the loss of solar electricity will surely lower our quality of life, forcing us to pedal our old bicycles to generate a lot less electricity than we're used to using. Not to mention we could never lower the Shield, even for an instant, with all of the Earth radioactive, and it would be a real tragedy to lose all our wild animals and plants and never be able to touch a living planet again. Our prospects are bleak if the people of Earth are too traumatized by the Invaders' killings — as we can see Manda is — to care bout Faraday's problem."

"I have to tell people. . . ." Tom got up from the table and joined the Yellowood Crew, all talking passionately at once at the sparkling Screen. Lizzy joined him, to translate.

▼

After sixty-seven hours, proposals and counter proposals, and two more sunrises for the people of Lane County, an Earth full of exhausted humans finally reached a series of agreements with the *Final Clones* led by Bill McClevy:

▼

FINAJ KONSENTO 97.4%

(FINAL CONSENSUS 97.4%)

(printed in English for the Faradayans, and in
Esperanto for the People of Earth)

▼

* **1)** The invaders would disarm themselves, sending ALL their weapons, without exception— from nukes to pistols — into the sun. (This was possible only because all the Colonels were dead.)

▼

* **2)** The starship would be moved from **L2**, behind the moon, to **L1**, between the Earth and the moon, and be prepared—by the Faradayans—for the people of Earth to take possession, rename it *TeroOni* (EarthOne), and return the Invaders home, in cryosleep, to Faraday.

▼

* **3)** No attempt would be made by the people of Earth to identify which soldiers had actually killed anyone on Earth. Earth acknowledges there can really be no realistic compensation made for the deaths of people, animals, or crops on Earth during the Invasion, except:

▼

* **4) All women, without exception, who were kidnapped by the Invaders will be returned to Earth.** Earth would expect most of those women will be alive. The bodies of any women, or *herms* (taken by accident because they had breasts, probably killed as 'monsters' when their hermaphroditic genitals were discovered) who died will also be returned, with their in-body ovaries <u>absolutely intact</u>. Failure to comply completely will void the deal. The Invaders were made to understand that all the women (and herms) captured must be returned, because <u>every Earther</u> had people who knew they had been kidnapped or killed. <u>No human on Earth</u> was anonymous or unknown. The Faradayans could collect no ovaries by deceit.

▼

 * **5)** The Earth crew of *TeroOni* would *control utterly* the ovaries—donated by living women left behind on Earth—which will be brought along for Faradayan reproduction.

▼

The first five Agreements were written and agreed on jointly by the People of Earth and the Final Clones of the Invasion Force. The last five were kept essentially secret (except in vague, inaccurate outline) from the Invaders:

▼

 * **6)** The Faradayans will be told that Earth's starship-crew consists only of men. Even the *Final Clones*—who will help the volunteers from Earth before they themselves are cryo-frozen—will be told that the crew will be entirely male, (to *utterly* protect the earthwomen — and the herms — in the crew from the grave danger of Faradayan murder, kidnapping, or enslavement.)

Faraday will be informed that if Faradayans Invade the starship, the ovaries will be immediately cremated.

If Faraday acquires human females, even only one, from elsewhere in the galaxy, *TeroOni* will immediately leave orbit and return to Earth.

If Faraday discovers there are women on board *TeroOni*, the starship will leave and return to Earth.

▼

* 7) Volunteers from Earth: women, herms, men and transpeople — people who had desired to explore space, and had long questioned why Earth had no deep space program — would crew the starship, considering themselves as still the people of Earth; villagers of the renamed starship, *TeroOni* Village; and they will farm the interior of the starship as they would the soil of Earth.

They will take with them ovaries volunteered by living women back on Earth so the burden of reproduction for Faraday will not fall on the living women in the crew of *TeroOni*.

Baby boys will be created by combining earth-eggs with sperm from specific Faradayan men, incubated on *TeroOni*, raised until the age of seven in an egalitarian atmosphere, *in a special area apart from the women and the herms*. Fathers will be given the opportunity to meet, by comscreen, their sons as they grow on *TeroOni*, so the boys will not be emotionally traumatized by their eventual removal down to live their lives with the men of Faraday.

For as long as the Meetings of Earth deem necessary, communicating with the starship by ansible, Faraday will be given no girls to enslave. They will only be given boys, so that Faraday will remain dependent on *TeroOni* alone for new, not cloned, genomes until such time as the culture of Faraday is sufficiently egalitarian and non-misogynist so that the people of Earth will feel positive about allowing them to have girls of their own.

It will be necessary to medically conquer the virus or prion which caused such demented xenophobia in the planet's past. Faraday's Racism must somehow be made to disappear. Many understand it will also be necessary to rid Faraday of the highly competitive economic system of capitalism—and its nasty ideology—before an egalitarian culture can grow and develop.

The complete re-vamping of the Faradayan culture will no doubt take centuries, so procedures must be put in place to relieve the *TeroOni* Villagers and their children (NOT the Faradayan children) so those who preferred to return to Earth may do so, and those interested in revamping Faradayan culture could be engaged in doing so. The details still needed to be worked-out.

▼

* 8) The people of Earth crewing *TeroOni* will be in contact with Earth itself by ansible, "tuned" so that messages from *TeroOni* to Earth and back cannot be "overheard" on Faraday. *(Actually, the electrons entangled with each other will only be in the TeroOni ansible and in the ansibles of Earth, not in any way entangled with any ansibles on Faraday.)*

▼

* 9) A light year — bout six trillion miles —is the distance the photons (quanta) of electromagnetic radiation — such as visible light, radio waves, X rays, etc — can travel in a vacuum, in a year, at 186, 282+ miles per second [the *'Speed of Light'*].

▼

*10) The yellow-white star which Faraday orbits, Delta Pavonis, is 19.9 light years from Earth. The starship will take 100 years (Earth time) to get there at reasonable sublight speeds.

17

▼

THE STARSHIP

The Faradayan starship was moved from Lagrange Point **L2** behind the moon by its pilots— both of them Final Clones — to **L1** between the Earth and the moon. Then McClevy and his men waited for the Earthers to come to the starship and claim it for Earth.

Peasant-Earth's 'manned' space program had, in fifteen hundred years, never progressed out from Earth-orbit to even the Moon. Earth's primary concern during all that time since the Final War had been in feeding people and in using science and technology to improve the freedom, peace, comfort, safety, and stability of human life on Earth.

The Space Collective had never been able to free-up enough resources to do anything other than to maintain the communication satellites. This had severely aggravated many people who were afraid their peaceful culture was stagnating because Earth's people were too deeply concerned with Recovery, and were not quickly expanding out into the solar system and ultimately the near-star-systems of the Milky-Way Galaxy.

Meanwhile, many humans with an itch for exploration and a yearning for contact with alien intelligence had spent those fifteen hundred years exploring the oceans of Earth and making friends with dolphins and whales (the sapient aliens close at hand). A spinoff technical breakthrough of the Ocean-Investigators' Syndic had led to the development of Stasis Technology, proving that scientific exploration is never totally useless.

When the Earth's first 'primitive' shuttle locked onto the Starship,

Bill McClevy sent Arnold Bates, the tall red-headed Private he had promoted to Corporal, to greet the arriving Earthers and officially turn the Starship over to Earth's control.

From Bate's viewpoint, a strange looking, very dark-skinned human in a bright red jumpsuit trimmed in royal purple — male of course — jaunted slowly out of the wide mouth of the tube from the shuttle docked at one end of the spinning Starship tube. They were at the axis of the Starship's spinning lumen, in free fall. The Earther held the pole of a black flag in his left hand. Occasional bright rainbow colors peeked out from the flag's folds. He stopped his forward motion easily by grabbing a thick braided strap, one of many trailing out from the entrance tube's mouth. A member of Earth's Space Collective, he was obviously skilled in free fall.

"Welcome to Starship FMC 2998 RR," Bates said to the Earther.

"Thank you, the strange dark-coloured man said. "Do you, umm, relinquish command?"

"Yes. Are you the proper authority?"

Bates was startled as the dark man's smile blazed bright in his black face. "Aye," the Black man said, "since I arrived in here first, I am the senior person of Earth aboard, so the honor is mine."

"Then the starship is yours."

"Let's go to the floor down there," the Black man said, pointing in the direction of the starship's cultivatable land, a green blur five miles away from the center of the lumen where they floated in free fall. "Come on," he gestured behind him to a small crowd of men, all in red jumpsuits, whose skin colours varied from tan to black. Bates led them to a small elevator where they all crowded in tightly, apparently unfazed by the close quarters. In less than a minute, they all burst out into the lumen. Bates was among them, dizzy from the unexpected close contact with the strange dark men he had trouble thinking of as fully and exactly human.

They were down on the floor (the land) of the long spinning lumen. Switching the flag to his right hand, the Black man strode with confidence out onto the grassy surface, surrounded by the other Earthmen. He speared the ground with the sharp end of the pole. "I claim this land for the people of Earth! This starship's name is now

TeroOni!" he announced loudly to the land which spread out in front
of them, curving up and over everyone's heads around the shining
suntube as the spinning starship pushed their feet firmly down onto the
grass-covered wall of the lumen. The self-appointed 'senior' Earthman
reached up and spread out the flag, revealing a wide rainbow-colored
stripe undulating horizontally across the black cloth. The other dark-
skinned earthmen cheered, and began to dance around the flag, singing
with enthusiasm in a strange language. With their diversity of non-
white skin colours, to Bates the dancing Earthers hardly seemed like
real human beings. He shivered with . . . was it *fear?*. . . Xenophobia?
Well, certainly, he was uncomfortable with the strange ceremony and
the strange '*people.*'

▼

Meanwhile in rooms and corridors beneath the land of the lumen
were all those Faradayan soldiers who had refused to work with the
Earthers, and who had survived protesting the destruction of all of
Faraday's weapons. Those uncooperative soldiers—who had been held
in very crowded conditions temporarily in the brig—were being put
into cryo-sleep to be awakened in 100 years on Faraday. Most of them
did not trust the Earthers would refrain from harming them while they
slept, and they had to be forcibly persuaded into the cryo-vaults. That
was proving to be difficult since all weapons had already been sent on
a trajectory into the sun.

Sergeant Keith Richardson was being man-handled by a squad of
large, over-muscled Final Clone soldiers with Bill McClevy in charge.

"Arrgh! Bill, you god-damned Traitor!. You let those Losers beat
us! How could you?" Richardson howled.

"The only way the Colonels could 'win' the Invasion," Bill told
him, "was to destroy the Earth and probably kill all the women. Now,
Sergeant, we've got a workable solution to our serious reproduction
problem, and the Earth, our natal planet, will live," Bill told him.

"No! Those pussy-whipped Earthers will totally control the
output from their ovaries!" Richardson snarled. "You've given those

god-damned *Losers power* over us!" He waved his arms, impeding efforts to start an IV.

"Strap him down, Boys; he ain't gonna hold still! So, Keith. We'll get the sons we need," Bill said softly, trying to sooth his old sex-buddy. "You know Faraday faces extinction."

"Bill, Lover, how can you—a super-educated man—dare to trust those filthy Earthers? They're stupid Peasants!"

"No, Keith, obviously they're not," Bill McClevy answered.

Davidson, the former Colonels' Moderator—unable to shake the lingering sense of responsibility he felt concerning the men he had formerly commanded—came along at that moment and commented, leaning close to Richardson so he was sure to be heard: "Well, Soldier, the Earthers <u>are</u> peasants, farmers, and apparently proud of it. But they're *not* stupid."

"Faraday won't allow the Earthers to have total control over our — *our!* — reproduction," Richardson howled. "You're in for a lot of trouble if we make it home!"

18

▼

PEASANTEARTH

Once they were sure the terrible weapons were gone and the Invasion was over, the partnership engineers at Yellowood and Rosebud Farms turned off their shared EnergyShield; and the crews of the two Earthships® began to clean up their farms from the destruction of the Invaders' mini-tanks.

Their animals remained under canopies alongside and *on* K-96 since both farms had to rebuild their outbuildings. Rosebud had to replace a large henhouse in what had been a grove of Mulberry trees, now destroyed, and Yellowood their blown-up cob-barn.

Manda Dighton, George W.C. Healy, and Jill Utica from Yellowood, plus Pak Hill, Zenobia Dighton, and Illie Martinsdale from Rosebud Farm took two horse wagons into Dighton Village to a warehouse to get pre-cut lumber — from Woodworks Farm six miles northwest of Dighton, which cultivated, harvested, and partially processed trees for construction-wood for all of Lane County — to rebuild the field fences and the barn stalls of Yellowood. The communards were also going to bring back many bags of clay and sharp sand to make cob to build anew the lost outbuildings of Yellowood and Rosebud Farms.

▼

Since they were hard-working farm people, the cob-builders started early in the morning, gathering soon after dawn in the area of Yellowood's ruined exterior garden and the barnyard north of the barn's ruins. People come from miles around, even Scott, Ness, Rawlins, and Graham counties, for the community fun of stomping and smooshing cob. Workers joined them from Pinklight Farm, which had no outbuildings (just an Earthship® with an interior, windowless, pink-lit grow space under the extra large northern-berm), and Grasshopper Farm, which expected help rebuilding their only cob house where they grew and processed grasshoppers to supply little crunchy tubes of protein to all the people of Lane, Ness, and Scott Counties. The Invaders had crisped their supply of grasshoppers, and Grasshopper Farm was waiting for replacement stock from *Akridoj Bieno* (Grasshopper Farm) near Lanxhou Village in the former nation of China, which had prudently included their grasshopper house under the protection of their Farm-Shield, and were thus prepared to re-supply less farsighted farmers of insects anywhere in the world.

Dillon Ness explained to Tom and several eager children how the work would go: "Okay, folks. Listen up. We're going to mix a classic cob recipe with our bare feet." Cheering, the children jumped up and down. "Will mix three of these buckets of sharp sand," he said, emptying the first bucket onto a six by eight foot tarp spread on the ground in a slight depression. "Okay. Two more buckets of sand. One bucket of finely ground red clay — we like the natural color — and a bucket of water. Make a depression for the water in the mound of dry material—like that. If we had river water nearby we'd use it, but here will use untreated rainwater. Variations of this recipe and this construction material have been in use for thousands of years by our ancestors all over the Earth. There are cob buildings still with us which are themselves many hundreds of years old, because they were built so well to start with. Cob buildings will generally last nearly a thousand years, if inhabited. Like living things, if abandoned, they dry out and crumble to dust."

The Yellowood Crew prepared several tarps for all the volunteer cobbers.

Musicians with fiddles, banjos, drums, and flutes were standing by to facilitate cob stomping. The toe-tapping music began.

▼

Tom — now called *Faraday*, because that was where he was *from* — was bare-chested and barefoot, wearing an old pair of Sheldon's trousers rolled above his knees. He joined the children enthusiastically stomping on a mound of clay, sand, and water. "Mix 'til all the grey sand disappears into the red clay," Ora Dighton told them. "Then will roll the mixture into a log shape with the tarp." She moved on to advise the next tarp-full of eager workers.

The muddy mixture squeezed between Tom's toes. He was surprised he was enjoying himself so much. There was nothing intellectual about the activity. His immediate companions were children, not all of them boys. A few of the smaller children wore no clothing at all. Tom found the little girls very strange.

Lizzy, wearing short shorts and a muscle-shirt, joined Tom's mostly-children group and got everyone to hold hands as they danced and stomped.

Periodically, everyone got off the reddish *muddy sand mixture* (not yet fully cob) and they rolled the mass of near-cob back and forth with the tarp into a log shape. Then the 'log' was covered with straw and — straw and more straw — stomped into the mixture until it was thick enough to form up by hand into a bread-loaf shaped glob which was classic *cob*, an ancient, strong, and completely reliable building material, a *super*-adobe.

A line was formed, including most of the older children, and everyone handed the cob '*loafs*' from person to person a short distance to the area where the cob barn was rising.

"A cob-building needs good 'feet' as well as a good 'hat'," Dillon Ness told them, continuing his instructional lecture on how to build with cob. "That is, a sturdy, waterproof, overhanging roof, which will get to later. The Invaders—sure by accident—left intact most of the rock foundation of our old cob barn, set firmly into the ground on a bed of gravel to help draw water away from the building's 'feet.' That, and the overhanging 'hat' roof will keep the cob walls dry because dripping or standing water can 'melt' cob."

An enthusiastic group of newcomers relieved Tom, Lizzy, and the children, and they went over to the barn foundation to help build one of the walls. Other groups were raising other walls, including the thick thermal mass dividing the horse and the cow/chicken sections of the barn.

Lizzy demonstrated how to *throw* the cob loaf down *hard* onto the rock foundation. She suggested that the smaller children were neither strong enough nor coordinated enough to throw cob down, and that they wait until the cob was on the foundation before they would poke holes with their fingers or a stick to prepare the cob to combine best with the next layer of 'loaf' thrown down upon it, making the finished wall one solid structure.

One of the older children showed Tom how to poke holes in the cob thrown onto the wall. Tom soon felt the simple pleasure and the satisfaction of creating a useful building with his (*muddy!*) hands in community with other human beings. They worked all morning, adding wooden frames for windows and doors—and the internal wooden walls of stalls, firmly held on one side in the cob—as they built up the cob walls.

Dillon continued to lecture: "Sharp sand, rather than smooth sand, clicks together to provide a stronger structure. The straw helps too. We use long stem straw—grown locally of course—to make the cob walls firm and essentially all one piece, like a large ceramic pot."

With so many people working, by a late lunchtime the Workers had built all the walls — complete with plumbing and electrical wiring, with barn doors and windows — up to the roof line.

Bekky Shields — still the food-cord for Yellowood Farm — had prepared a special buffet lunch in the GatherRoom for her shipmates and the visiting workers. Everyone washed their hands and feet before eating.

Well away from other people and the building site, the smaller children—all of them now nude, squealing with delight—squirted each other with hoses until they were mostly mud free, which was great fun in the last heat of summer. Elder Jameka Lunawanna sort-of supervised. She avoided soaking herself as best she could. The children, mindful of her age, were careful with her. The implied responsibility helped calm them down.

Filling for the fish sandwiches had come from Fisher Farm, a mile west of the border with Ness County on K-96. Fisher Farm grew fish in tall *stay*glass tanks in large thick-walled turret-shaped fish houses, with *stay*glass roofs, directly connected to the east and west sides of their Earthship®. Unlike Yellowood and Rosebud Farms, they had years ago designed their FarmShield to cover their entire farm, so they were immediately able to share the products of their farm labor in the same manner as they always had. One of the visiting workers wore a fish shaped pin on the neck of her T-shirt to brag of her crew-status at Fisher Farm, and many people thanked her — on behalf of her home farm — for the fish.

▼

After lunch, the ad-hoc cob builders raised the barn-roof of parallel wood beams and covered it with shake shingles until the roof was overhanging the cob walls. The younger children were disappointed they couldn't help with the roof [adults were afraid of children falling], so they were set to work decorating the barn's exterior walls with bas-relief sculptures of thick adobe: imaginary fire breathing dragons; herds of elegant, galloping horses; cows with large milk-filled udders; *ducks* (secretly encouraged by Sheldon Rozel, as part of his years-long campaign to add ducks to Yellowood's animal population); and chickens (sitting hens and roosters crowing). Adults helped them sculpt and paint the bas-relief sculptures in beautiful colors.

After the roof was set and the barn was water-tight, the Workers applied a *near-cob* plaster of straw dust, lime, water, sharp sand, and pale clay to the interior walls, and laid a red cob floor in both halves of the barn. Then they placed electric heaters inside to help cure and dry the floor and walls as the sun would on the outside. When it began to rain, they crowded together into the Yellowood Earthship®'s greenhouse corridor and cheered when it was clear the new roof of the cob barn was doing its all-important job.

▼

That evening, after supper, Tom took Lizzy aside and asked her to go with him back to Faraday. "I'll take care of you," he said. "We could have a good life. You can continue your Anthropology studies at Clarke

University, and eventually teach. You don't have to be a farmer all your life. You could be an academic, like me."

"I *am* a farmer. I like being a farmer," she said, frowning. "Oh, Bob, Torrin, Sheldon, Jill. Could you come here a minute?" When her older Shipmates came over, she told them what Tom had asked.

"Tom, we're sorry. You can't leave Earth," Bob told him, his voice thick with concern and compassion.

"What? Why?" Tom sputtered.

"Because you know, as does everyone on Earth, there will be women on Starship *TeroOni*. Can you see the danger to them if Faraday knew they were aboard?"

"I want to go home!" Tom cried. "My whole life is back there on Faraday. I have a teaching position at Clarke University. My best friend is returning. I can protect Lizzy!—"

"'Women on Starship *TeroOni*' is too big and important a secret for you to carry alone, Tom," Torrin said, "and we can't trust you to keep it—*or to really understand the desperate importance of keeping it*—alone for the rest of your life. Don't you understand what you saved Manda from?"

"But—"

"And I wouldn't go with you, Tom," Lizzy said. *"I am a farmer,* and I want to farm here at Yellowood, in Lane County, on my planet Earth, for the rest of my life. I chose this years ago."

"Remember, Tom, there are no women on Faraday," Jill said. "Only on Earth can you have a sex life with a real woman. Believe me, I understand that need. And you have a woman here who wants to be your lover. Right?" Jill asked Lizzy, who nodded. "Why not stay with us? Nicodemus Village in Graham County has JohnBrown University not too far north of us, where you could teach, and come down often to visit Lizzy. Or if you want—because you brought Manda back to us— you can join the shipmates here at Yellowood Earthship®, which you are welcome to do—Right?" she asked the other communards.

"Aye," Dillon said—he had walked up and joined the group—and the other Seniors agreed in chorus.

"And Tom, you and I could have two children, a boy and a girl, one of each traditional gender to replace us in Earth's population,"

Lizzy said. "The Dighton BirthHouse techs could make two embryos from the best combinations of our genomes that are possible. And the children would grow up healthy here, at Yellowood Farm. Whether or not you go to Nicodemus to teach. We could be lovers for a long time, I feel. I'm not polyamorous nor the casual type."

"How could you trust me? I want to join the Starship. . . ."

"Our Space Collective has been alerted. You won't get into Space, Tom," Dillon said. "We People of Earth know how important it is that Faraday never know there are women astronauts."

"Don't let them go if it's so dangerous!" Tom exclaimed.

"You want us to discriminate on the basis of gender against people who have longed for deep-space all their lives? Deny them just because they're women?" Sheldon asked.

"If you stay, Tom," Lizzy snapped, "you'll have to get rid of your automatic desire to discriminate against people for the sake of your personal convenience."

"But if it's dangerous . . ."

"Adult humans, *any* adult humans, may chose danger, hard work, or anything else for themselves, and no one has a right to prevent that free choice by a free person, as long as they're not trying to hurt other people," Bob Beiler told him.

"Hey, Tom," Jill said, touching his shoulder. "Stay, be a university professor, create children with Lizzy, and be her lover. Not a bad situation for you. Avoid one hundred cold years of cryosleep returning to a society where you ain't really free — seems to me — and where you will never again have the chance to make love with a real woman."

"But why can't the men of Faraday know there are women on *TeroOni?*" Tom bleated.

The other communards had been gathering around as the discussion grew louder. Aisha McHenry replied, "Because the men of Faraday don't consider women to be people, eh? But rather as *things* to be used, controlled, and owned by men as property.

"Before the Final War, that misogynous belief was quite common on Earth, despite over three centuries of feminist activism by both women and men, but our post-War-culture got over it long ago. Women on Faraday would never be seen as equal people . . . but, uh . . . Yall men of Faraday actually do *not* have equality among yourselve*s*, do you, eh?"

Tom was quiet for a long time. The Yellowood shipmates stood quietly and gave him time to think.

"All right!" he said at last. "You won't let me go home? Not even if I give you my word?"

"We can't risk it, Tom," Jill said softly. "It would be catastrophic if Faraday found out women — whom they don't consider to be people worthy of equal treatment — are on board *TeroOni*. I shudder at the thought of being treated like a very valuable *thing*."

"Yes!" Tom said, suddenly understanding. "You would always be a very valuable *thing* if the children you produced were pale-skinned enough." Disgusted, he twitched his head irritably.

"So stay, Tom," Lizzy continued. "Stay and learn how great it is to be a free person in Solidarity with other free people. You and I will make children together. . . . You can teach Anthropology. . . . Oh, frack-it, accept the inevitable, Tom, and learn to be a happy man!"

"I'm, uh, sorry," Dillon told him, "but we had to confiscate that phone you were using to talk to your friend, uh, Bill? On the Starship. We can't take any chances. Once *TeroOni* is gone, we will give you a personal adult eTabb you can't use to contact the starship. But you *can* use it on Earth, as a phone and a Net-Library interface. You can program it to let you know whenever something or an exhibit you're interested in is coming up near where you live, or anything else. Education is for everyone. You see? Everyone on Earth is connected to the greatest parts of our culture, anytime, all the time."

"All right," Tom said tightly.

"You know will keep you under constant surveillance til the Starship leaves, don't you?" Dillon asked.

"Yes, I understand," Tom sighed.

▼

Lizzy's bedroom was typical of all Earthships®. Although a single room, it had a double- wide bed (in case of company), as well as a graywater planter against the southern, tall *stay*glass wall shared with the greenhouse corridor. It was bursting with Lizzy's choice of edible greenery: lush grapevines, thick with green leaves, heavy with clusters of fat, purple, concord grapes, weaving around a wood trellis.

All the thermal-mass walls of the room were made of old rubber tires packed with rammed earth, plastered smooth with near-cob adobe layered over concrete. Across from the foot of the bed was a wide, tall, wooden bookcase filled with Lizzy's anthropology and architecture books. She admitted her collection was old fashioned, but she liked books she could hold in her hands, rather than computer entries. The wall above her bed held pictures of humans Lizzy said were her 'Family', the crew of the Earthship® on Merlot Farm where she had been raised. Tom was relieved to learn that 'family' also included her genetic parents. The crew of Yellowood had already told him of stranger arrangements. For instance, Manda was considered to have been 'twins' with another woman who was not related to her at all, and both of them had been parented, as 'twins', by two men who were also not blood-related to either of them. And Jill Utica had created a daughter with Legacy-Sperm from a dead man. Tom thought she was attractive enough to interest any living man.

Lying together in bed, Lizzy gladly talked to him about her childhood family. "My genetic parents are Mira Horni-Briza, who grew up in the former Czech Republic in Europe, and Omar Yendi, from the former nation of Ghana on the African Continent. They got together when she was forty-five, he forty —"

"Your mother had you when she was over forty-five years old?" Tom was surprised.

"Well, her ovary was in stasis since she was a young teen. I explained bout our BirthHouses and replicant-wombs, didn't I?"

"I'm just surprised your parents were middle aged . . ."

"With our average life spans of 130 years, forty five is not middle aged. Bob-&-Dillon in their early sixties are early middle aged. And we've learned that life partnerships are stronger and last longer when the people involved have had a chance to 'sow their wild oats,' — as the old-fashioned saying goes — grow to true maturity, mellow, and get to know themselves and the kind of people they most enjoy being with long term. Our genetic material is always young, kept in stasis."

"Okay. Not a bad idea, I guess." he said.

"I learned a lot from both my parents. Mom would often lead us shipmates in song when we had communal work to do. She's an expert with her mandolin. Dad often accompanies her with a small hand drum. He also gave me my interest in anthropology, and taught me a lot bout cooking. Mom is a horse whisperer like Sheldon is. Merlot Farm has a few horses, as do most farms. Great animals. I ride *Noktomezo* over every few months — Merlot Farm is a little bit east by southeast of us here — to see them both, the rest of my old family, my former shipmates, to catch up, have dinner, celebrate their latest batch of wine, listen to Mom play her new five-string banjo. Lately, she's taken that up."

"Why's your last name Alamota?"

"Cause I was incubated in a replicant womb in the Alamota Village BirthHouse. The custom, generally in North America — and also where my parents grew up — is for us to take our last names from the village — the place where we were incubated and were born, that is, *decanted* — serving the area where we were raised. That way no two living people have the exact same name."

"That's interesting," he said.

"I did meet another Lizzy once," she said smiling, reminiscing, "while I was in the Amazon Basin on my YouthTrip. Lizzy Oshcosh she was, from Oshcosh Village in Winnebago County in North America on the *Volpo* River where it enters Lake Winnebago. She said it barely missed being nuked during the *Final War* because it was right next to, and partly intermingled with, the small city of Oshcosh, of the same name. She told me that over the centuries since the Final War, they dismantled that city and recycled its parts, making a big park out of it on the bank of the Volpo River. She learned to sail small boats on Lake Winnebago, and still does, like all the kids in Oshcosh Village. They have regattas. Lizzy-O said the races are fun to sail, or to watch.

"Lizzy-O and I call each other and talk, every once in a while. Lizzy-O and Lizzy- A, the Lizard Sisters, we sometimes joke."

"I've been meaning to ask," Tom said. "Umm . . . what did Jill mean when she said she could understand my need to have sex with a real woman?"

"Oh, Jill is a Lesbian."

"What's that?"

"Don't folks on Faraday recognize the inherent existence of homosexuals?"

"Sure, my best friend Bill —"

"A Lesbian is a woman who is homosexual."

"What? How? I mean, how could two women have sex without a man?"

"Mean, without a penis?"

"Well . . . yeah."

"Two women can do together whatever, say, you and I could do that doesn't involve your penis."

"Oh. I don't think I would like that."

"Neither would I, which is why I'm not a Lesbian."

"I'm glad."

"But, Tom, if you're going to live here with me, even part time, Jill is now going to be your shipmate, so you'll have to be, uh . . . like a brother to her, and not think anything at all bout her sex life."

"Oh . . . Okay."

19

▼

PEASANT-EARTH

Before the Invasion, all the people of Earth had known there were bright, happy futures ahead for each of them. So after the problem with the Invaders was solved, the Earthers — almost all of them ordinary people interested only in being ordinary people —returned to their semi-Utopian lives, filled with the promise of living safe, not adventurous nor dangerous lives, enjoying their useful, satisfying work, in the company of family and friends; periodically celebrating the cycles of life.

That was all the vast majority of humanity had ever wanted. And Peasant-Earth had adventures enough for those few human beings who desired danger and exciting experience. In the wilderness, wild animals and their environments needed to be monitored by humans unarmed except with their wits, so unusual catastrophes did not drive into extinction rare, much beloved, potentially useful, or interesting animals and plants. Research continued in the wilderness of Earth's oceans with the sapient '*aliens*' of Earth — whales and dolphins.

Extreme sports (such as long-distance hang-gliding, orbit-diving, and mountain-climbing) or unpleasantness-free competitions (such as horse-racing, sailing regattas, and global olympics) occupied the recreational-time of many who hungered for adventure outside of natural science.

Even Manda, despite her ongoing grief over losing Suzie, realistically expected to live for many years on Earth exactly as she herself chose, probably as one of the 89% of the Earth's population involved in farming. Like most people, she wanted an ordinary life, working at a job which interested her, falling in love, reproducing, watching her children grow up, spending her old age among beloved family and friends, comfortably and usefully. . . .

▼

Several weeks after the Yellowood Shipmates and their neighbors had built their new cob-barn, Manda was in her Earthship®'s kitchen helping Bekky make cheese so Yellowood could reduce the excess supply of milk building up in their stasis cupboards.

Three of Yellowood's dairy cows would soon have to be retired to pasture — they were getting too old to have another calf and give milk — so the communards had added a seventh and an eighth cow to their small dairy herd.

Bob Beiler waited patiently while Manda poured a large, warm pan full of curds and whey through cheesecloth to separate them. That task over, she habitually glanced around, and then sighed miserably because Suzie would never be in sight again.

"Manda," Bob said. "We just got a call that Suzie's body has been found in Mobile Bay—just off the Caribbean, near where the Tombigbee River enters the bay—by fishers from Daphne Village."

Manda stood up eagerly, and then sat down again, sadly realizing that Bob's news didn't mean she was really going to see her 'twin' again. "How are they sure it's her?" she asked.

"DNA. They're sending her body back to us in a sealed coffin. Can have a funeral at the SouthWest Corner Cemetery in Dighton when it finally arrives. And investigators from that Intentional Jewish Community, in Marengo County where yall were headed, found yall's backpaks and bicycles, yall's eTabbs smashed, and some clothes." Bob put his giant hand on top of hers on the prep table.

"Thanks, Dad," she said, patting his hand. "*B'nai Khesed*, that's the place." She put her head down on the table, too head-achy and depressed to cry.

▼

Later that day, Manda called that Intentional Jewish Community in the former state of Alabama to thank them for finding her and Suzie's belongings.

"Hello, Tikva Farm, **B'nai Khesed** Community, Marengo County. Rachael Rosenberg speaking." An attractive young woman in her late thirties with mahogany coloured skin and curly black hair repeated her greeting in *Esperanto: ("Saluton"),* and then apparently in Hebrew: *("Shalom").*

"Oh, hi," Manda said. "I'm calling from Yellowood Farm in Lane County on the Great Plains, to thank yall folks for finding the backpaks and bicycles we lost when my twin was . . . *kih* . . . *killed* by the Invaders and I was kidnapped. You might have heard the story. I spoke of it during the global eMeet last September, when we decided what to do bout the Invaders."

"Aye! Remember. You're the one that Invader soldier rescued, and brought back to Earth."

"Aye. When you think bout where he came from, what he did was amazing. I was too much of a wreck at the time to fully realize it. Just instinctively trusted him. He felt like an island of decency in the midst of that hell I was trapped in."

"Whatever happened to him, d'you know? The Invaders must have charged him with Treason, for daring to rescue you."

"They did. He stayed with us. He's partnered with one of my shipmates, Lizzy Alamota.

"We've come to love him, but he's not really a very good farmer. He spends part of his time in Nicodemus Village in Graham County, teaching Anthropology at JohnBrown University. Nicodemus and JohnBrown U—am not sure you know," Manda continued—"were founded by ex-slaves who fled the war-torn ex-Confederate South after the USA's Civil War long ago in the nineteenth century."

"Never knew that. You're up on your local history, ain't you?

"Aye. Most folks are, hmm?"

"So how've you been, Manda?" Rachael asked. "Twins is an unusual relationship these past fifteen centuries, what with replicant-wombs and genetic selection."

"Suzie and I weren't genetically related. Just decanted on the same day. And because we had the same birthday, people at our farm always called us 'the twins'. We liked it. We, uh . . . ukk . . . we . . . always meant to live our lives to*gether*, raise our children together. Maybe in your community. She said her eggmother was Jewish."

"Yall weren't raised by yall's genetic parents?"

"No, both the pairs, our gene-parents, were really young, in their very early twenties, and their romantic partnerships didn't last."

"Not unusual," Rachael said.

"But we had Primary Parents at Yellowood Farm," Manda continued. "Two great guys, partners Bob-&-Dillon, older, steadier, so we had a solid growing up. Yellowood is a great farm. Dighton is a great village, with great schools. We . . . we were happy."

With the difficulties of the Invasion, the work of farming, and making many a round of cheese, Manda Dighton had been very busy since she returned to Yellowood Farm. Suzie's funeral was a difficult time to get through. She leaned heavily on her shipmates. She needed the love.

The pain of losing Suzie was fading slowly, except for those times when she lay alone in their former shared bed and needed to tell her twin about some part of her day. She still often went to sleep at night with tears in her eyes, but tried not to bother anyone else. (Except, some nights, she crept into bed with Bob-&-Dillon, pretending she was still a child.)

She continued talking with the Jewish woman at Tikva Farm, *B'nai Khesed* Community, calling her once a week or so:

"Ah, Manda," Rachael said one day, "I'm glad . . ."

"What?"

"I'm glad to hear you tell such positive stories of your childhood with your 'twin'. I'm glad yall's childhoods were happy. . . ." She looked chagrined. "Manda, I left a small child in your part of the world, when I was very young, on my youth trip. How old are you?"

"Just turned twenty. Fracking miserable birthday, without Suzie."

"The child I left, uh . . . bout seventeen years ago, was a toddler-girl I had named Susan, a good Jewish name. At that time in my life, I hadn't fully connected with my Jewish Heritage, but I did know I was probably Jewish, and if I had a child, the child would be Jewish also, having my mitochondrial DNA—like my genetic mother's—so I gave her the only Jewish name I knew, other than my own. I've never known if I did the right thing to leave her."

"People do it all the time. We're all *Kids of the Farm.* Everybody gets Primary Parents. Works out. Umm, Suzie's and my gene-parents left when we were three. You might be Suzie's gene-mom. Will have to check the DNA."

"Aye. Aye! Let's talk bout how we could do that."

"Well, I could bring Suzie's ovary to your farm, and you could get your area's BirthHouse to check the DNA profile, see if it half-matches yours. Do you have a BirthHouse you use?"

"Of course. Our Intentional Jewish Community is spread out over several farms closely surrounding the Village of Half-Acre, so we think of the Village BirthHouse as ours — we share its facilities with anyone who needs them, of course — and we can get the DNA testing done there pretty quickly."

"Okay. And if you don't mind, being Suzie's mom would kinda make you my mom too, since Suzie and I were 'twins'. I've never had a mom, my Primary Parents being both men. I'd love to visit and tell you a lot more bout who Suzie was."

"That would be wonderful. I have a son with my partner here, but we've never made a girl. I always thought that'd be wrong since I already left a daughter behind. And two children a couple has been the standard for over a thousand years, so our population doesn't spike up and we don't overwhelm our resources. *Can* you come here?"

"Aye, uh course. And I can easily bring Suzie's ovary, rather than send it by air-mail post. She and I made each other our egg-heirs when we were young teens. We registered with the Dighton BirthHouse at the time of our operations. Do you do that in *B'nai Khesed?*"

"Oh, aye," Rachael said. "We're very modern here. We feel that returning to the Ages of Non-Personhood for Women is not really necessary to living Jewish lives together. We would call it—that is, returning to the chancy, old fashioned, male-controlled, more animal-natural method of reproduction—we would call it *Mitzraim*, the land of slavery, the Hebrew name for Egypt, also meaning Narrowness or Constraint."

She continued, "Jewish women have already come out the Bondage in Egypt—actually and metaphorically—and we have no desire to return to *any kind* of slavery."

"That's great," Manda said, "Umm, also, I need to ask, how yall folks there in **B'nai Khesed** Community get yall's last names. I couldn't find a listing for a Village named 'Rosenberg', anywhere in the world."

"Our custom is, we chose our last names — from Jewish people in the past whom we admire — when we accept our responsibilities as Jewish adults in Judaism — that's our community's religion — at the time of our b'nai mitzvah ceremonies, at twelve or thirteen, (or even later for people like me who had to find our way back to Jewish life). We become "Children of the Law" by reading before the Congregation from the traditional Torah scroll, which is handwritten in ancient Hebrew, without vowels, you know."

"Ah."

▼

A week later, on horseback, accompanied by many of her shipmates, Manda went right after breakfast one morning from Yellowood Farm to the Dighton BirthHouse to pick up Suzie's ovary. Then she and her shipmates went on through the village to the Annabella AirStation. After hugs and kisses all around, Torrin Beeler, Bekky Shields, Ora Dighton, Tom-&-Lizzy, and others returned to Yellowood, leading the horses the air-travelers had ridden.

Marsha-&-Sheldon, with their offspring (Anelia and Edgardo), plus Bob-&-Dillon, got on the solar-plane with Manda to go to the **B'nai Khesed** Community just north of the Caribbean.

▼

Kim Scott lived in an Earthship® commune in Dighton Village, on Eleventh Street near the AirStation, where they had a big kitchen which cooked for their AirTravel Syndic to provide food for air passengers flying out of Dighton.

Kim was no longer in training to be an air pilot. She had graduated. She was Captain for Manda's special trip eastward to Tikva Farm. Her new copilot-in-training, Yuri Yakutsk, was a dark-brown young man who deliberately spoke Ameriglish with a warm Russian accent, greeting everyone with a giant smile and sparkling black eyes, to honor his seed-father who had been born in Siberia where they still spoke Russian, and who had taught Yuri to speak Russian as a little child. He did the takeoff so well the passengers were unaware he had done it instead of Kim, until she told them.

While Yuri tended the autopilot as they cruised east by southeasterly, Kim encouraged everyone to have coffee, tea, or fruit juice. "Lunch is a while away, and the trip will take a few hours," she told them.

▼

Tense, Manda sat alone with Suzie's ovary in a stasis box in a cloth carry bag. Marsha sat down beside her with a mug of strawberry juice in hand. "Everything will be okay," she told Manda. "Just think of this as a continuation of your YouthTrip. We'll miss you, but you can come back to Yellowood anytime, if you like."

"I hope it's a lot better than my 'official' YouthTrip, which is *over*," Manda said. "I know I'll miss Yellowood, but I think life will be easier for me away from the place where Suzie and I grew up. If not *B'nai Khesed*, I thought I might go elsewhere: Europe, maybe to the island of Iceland, where all the Earthships® have double greenhouses, which interests me."

"Manda, I know Sheldon is really glad you let us come along with you." Marsha said.

"Well he's Jewish. . . ."

"And so are our kids, at least according to some Reform Jewish ideas developed two or three centuries before the *Final War*. If both parents ain't Jewish, doesn't have to be only the mother to make the kids Jewish. Can be just the father. I looked it up."

"Well, Sheldon always had Anelia and Edgardo help him host those Passover Dinners we had. They both chant really good in Hebrew, as

I remember. But I'm glad we all got a chance to cook. I loved making Sheldon's recipe for fluffy matza balls."

"So maybe a few things will be familiar to you on Tikva Farm in **B'nai Khesed** Community," Marsha said, smiling.

"Aye. Thanks, Marsha. I think I may be relaxed enough now to have a cup of coffee." Manda began to lever herself up.

"No, no. Sit still with your stasis box. Let me get you coffee," Marsha said.

▼

Bob-&-Dillon came over and sat with Manda.

"Hi, Dads," Manda said.

"We're gonna miss you honey," Dillon said.

"It won't be so bad, though, having you still on Earth," Bob said. "We were afraid you might decide to go with *TeroOni*."

"No! Oh, I don't mind the decision made by the global eMeet, to aid the Faradayans with their reproduction crisis. There seem to be enough safety procedures in place to keep Earth and Earth-women safe. But I *personally* would never lift a finger to help those God-fracked . . . *ukh*. They and all their mis . . . misogynist . . . racist, vi . . . vi . . . violent ideas should go extinct! . . . *Frack-it!* I can't seem to get over this rage. It debilitates me."

Dillon put his arms around her. He was careful with the stasis box containing Suzie's ovary. Bob stood up and put his arms around them both. "You've had more horror to deal with than most people have had over the last fifteen centuries, Sweetie," Bob told her. "Maybe you, a few mindmenders, and some other people who lost someone in the Invasion could get together by 3D maybe, and find a way to work-out your feelings. . . ."

▼

Lunchtime came at last, and the food, as always with the AirTravel Syndic, was delicious and vegetarian. Among the fresh fruits and vegetables, there were little peanut butter and fruit compote sandwiches, which delighted Manda. Then, since they were hardworking people who rarely had a day off from routine farm chores, they all stretched out in their seats, or in sleepsaks on the padded floor, for an afternoon nap.

Manda drowsed, her arms around the stasis box. She heard one of her fathers — Dillon — saying to Marsha:

"Tamir Branson from Greendale Farm—near Merlot Farm, where Lizzy's from—is the only person I know of from our area who's leaving with TeroOni."

"Thank the Goddess Lizzy didn't decide to go," Bob said.

Manda turned over in her semi-sleep, clutching the stasis box to her chest. She heard fragments of conversation:

"Earth people will go into cryo intermittently over 100 years so the original people—who personally remember Earth and the Agreements we all made through Interkonsento / Centra—will be alive and vigorous when the starship reaches Faraday. . . ."

"A newly formed global side-syndic of the Free Association of BirthHouse Workers, (the Libera Asocio Naskig Domo a Laboristoj [LANL] Collective), is going along to make sure all the Agreements bout the Ovaries are kept," someone else said.

"If the Faradayans try to invade the Starship, the Ovaries are toast."

Manda did not recognize the voice. *The co-pilot, Yuri?* She snoozed on . . .

"Time to get up everyone! We're nearly there," Kim called out.

People began stretching and yawning. Dillon was still asleep and snoring lightly. Manda left Suzie's stasis box with a fully-awake Bob Beiler, and dashed aft to the toilet facilities.

▼

Yuri landed them with no trouble and taxied toward the AirStation. On one side of the plane's dim interior, the outer door was obvious on the wall with its attached steps hanging upside down. The afternoon sun blazed suddenly through cracks as the door began to open. Its attached steps unfolded outward and down onto the tarmac. The sunlight seemed very bright.

Followed by her shipmates, Manda clutched Suzie's stasis box in its cloth tote as she walked to the top of the steps leading out of the solar-plane. She felt Bob-&-Dillon behind her, on each side, her fathers' hands solid and comforting on her shoulders. She took a deep breath. She was a little apprehensive as she thus entered into a new world, the beginning of her adult life, to be known to everyone she met from then on as a single, *un*-twinned person. She knew, in a sense, she was renewing her YouthTrip, so horribly interrupted by the Invasion.

A typically multi-coloured crowd of people waited below in the golden sunshine. Manda spied Rachael Rosenberg. Like all the others, a welcoming smile lit her face. As Manda started down the steps, they all shouted, gladly, and in unison: "**Shalom!**"

20

▼

THE STARSHIP

In *TeroOni*, the Earthers found the Land of the lumen had been used by the Faradayans for war practice. When all of them were sitting in a circle on the Land, they discussed their communal problems in a strange language.

Bates—who spoke several Earth languages—felt he could occasionally recognize a word or two. Bates learned languages as easily as some men breathed. His progenitor had been a valuable servant, a translator for the Elites.

The Earthers complained to Bates—in chaotic combinations of Ameriglish, Cantonese, and Swahili, with a touch of Yiddish—that because the Land had been so badly used for mock violence, there was *way* too much work to do to ready it for its first crops.

Bates talked to McClevy, and the Faradayans formed teams with the remaining soldiers (mostly Final Clones) to go over the land carefully inch by inch to pick up trash, oil slicks, unexploded gunpowder or its residue, remove combat installations, and repair damage to the turf. The men of Earth were shocked and then amused at the precise military way the Faradayans formed up to work. Was it necessary for a few of the men to yell so loudly at all the rest?

▼

When the cleanup was done, the Earthers began building a wall across the entire lumen, nine-point-five miles from one end. The Faradayans were told it was going to be for a CO_2-rich farm area, where the farmers would wear oxygen / nitrogen masks and the plants would flourish in an atmosphere best for them, not so good for humans. Bates—still fulfilling the role of liaison from the Faradayans to the Earthers—asked the Black-coloured man, the 'leader'—whose name was Elombe Caldwell—"Why are you-all doing that?"

"We Folk of Earth are the best farmers in the Galaxy, I'm sure," Elombe said. "Didn't we take a planet, the creation cradle of the whole human race — ruined by a devastating Nuclear War — and make it green and bountiful again, by collectively — on a planetary scale, in free Solidarity — applying science and hard work?"

"Faraday is today green and beautiful," Bates said. "But when our ancestors got there, the native vegetation was a sickly purple and red, without any green chlorophyll, totally incompatible with human life. So you see, humans succeed in surviving and prospering, wherever they go." Bates felt very strange to find himself arguing that Faradayans were *just as good humans as* . . . just as good as . . . *Earthers? . . . What?* Talking to Elombe, whom his Faradayan culture defined as a Loser, barely human—and with such dark skin—was often confusing, and somewhat frightening, to Bates.

"We," Elombe continued, "all the People of Earth, rural folk — farmers, most of us — survived, without forcing others, without forming people into lines, without yelling at each other, without violence."

"Um . . . uh . . . well . . . We all have our ways, now don't we?"

"I prefer freedom," Elombe said quietly, "and Solidarity."

"Depends on your definition," Bates said stiffly.

"There's been fifteen centuries of peace on Earth," Elombe said. "We have, in a sense, achieved the ancient human dream of Utopia. Except, the reality of the Universe is that '*The Only Constant is Change*'. Some would say — and I believe it's true, in a sense — that our culture on Earth has stagnated."

"No!" he was contradicted by another Earther nearby, a hefty man in a navy blue coverall with a bright orange-and-white-striped, collarless shirt, a man who also looked *very* dark-skinned to Bate's eye.

"Not stagnated," the dark, hefty Earther continued. "The *rate* of change is just slower, less dramatic, and less apparently fundamental than it was in the Elite-dominated eras, when there was so much force, privilege, and violence. For instance, the development of *stasis* almost a thousand years ago was a major triumph of scientific work. I mean, the conquest, in small specific spaces, on a human scale, of Entropy itself! What an achievement! We can halt Entropy! Stasis does so much better than salt or cold in preserving food, and also makes our modern reproductive-archiving possible. Plus, we spent most of our energy in scientific research over the centuries not on improving weapons of war — like you Faradayans — but on eliminating dangerous disease organisms from our planet."

"Well. . . ." Elombe said, "So — we of the Space Collective believe — if we do not want to basically change our Utopia on Earth — and we don't, Jem, we *don't!*" — he said, addressing the other Earther. "Then we must change and expand out into the galaxy. The 'small' volume around our Solar System, with our star named Sol — within a fifty light-year radius — is already populated by humans, so we can bring the *ideals* of our '*Utopia*', the freedom of our wonderfully civilized Anarkhy, rooted in Solidarity, to humans in other star systems. We'll start with Faraday," he said to Bates.

"That'll be tough, I can tell you," Bates said sadly. "Faraday has an authoritarian culture dominated by the military — and even though most people don't realize it — it is defined by militaristic ideals. Thinking on Faraday is controlled by the fantasy of authoritarian rule as superior to any other, by the so-called 'right-of-violence' to dominate, and by the idea that so-called efficiency and central-control are more important, and organize better, than messy human emotional needs."

"Will just have to wait and see what the next generation brings," Elombe said quietly.

21

▼

PEASANT-EARTH

Sheldon Rozel had returned to Yellowood Farm from the **B'nai Khesed** Community with his family to think-over whether or not he wanted to join the Jewish Intentional Community in Marengo County far to the east. One morning after breakfast he asked Tom to come along with him to deliver dairy products, berries, and some vegetables to neighboring farms and gather foodstuffs that Yellowood needed. "I'm kinda the unofficial food-gatherer for Yellowood Farm," Sheldon said in the barnyard as he began to hook up four horses to the farm's largest wagon. "Remember you and I stopped by Pinklight Farm for supplies the day you joined us?"

"Yeah, umm. . . aye," Tom said.

Wearing a wide-brimmed hat to give her face some shade under the sun, pale-skinned Bekky Shields came along too, for an outing, and to see what 'exotic' foodstuffs the Yellowood Crew could gather for use in her role as her shipmates' food-cord and chief cook. Her light-weight shirt was long-sleeved. She wore trousers.

At the last minute, Lizzy joined them too, saying she needed the time to continue Tom's lessons in current Earth Anthropology.

Because their next-door neighbors to the east, the shipmates of Grasshopper Farm, did not keep cows or goats, Yellowood delivered several *stay*glass bottles of delicious raw milk, three tubs of unsalted butter, and several rounds of cheese for Grasshopper's stasis cupboards. Bekky insisted they pick up a few final packages of last season's harvested grasshoppers, with wings, legs, ovipositors, and antennas removed, in stasis, which she liked to use as crunchy protein supplements in her casseroles. So soon after the Invasion, Grasshopper Farm had not yet received their eagerly awaited replacement stock of viable grasshoppers from Lanxhou Village in the former nation of China.

"On Faraday, we were never so desperate for food we had to eat *insects*," Tom remarked as they left Yellowood. He was sitting beside Sheldon as his new friend controlled the horses. Bekky and Lizzy were lounging behind them on the second padded seat of the wagon. Sacks of vegetables, packages of grasshoppers from Grasshopper Farm, and all the goods Yellowood had to share — milk, butter, cheese, vegetables, berries, and such, many in portable stasis cupboards — were arranged neatly in the bed of the wagon behind them. Also included were several sturdy bags of horse- or cow-manure, to share with farms who needed fertilizer for their gardens. The farmers of Yellowood, having several horses and milk-cows, always had more manure than they could possibly use.

"Grasshoppers and crickets are great sources of complete protein," Sheldon remarked. "Conveniently, most vegetarian folk have no trouble regarding insects as '*vegetables*' rather than animals."

"Were there grasshoppers in last night's casserole?" Tom asked.

"Nope," Sheldon said, grinning. He turned and winked at Bekky.

"Oh, good," Tom said.

"Crickets," Sheldon said, his grin widening.

"Oh! . . . I guess . . . uh, it's too late to throw up," Tom said.

Bekky chuckled.

Lizzy said, "Come on back here with us, Tom. I know you have lots more Anthropology questions, beginning with insects. Bekky can help me explain. She's much better educated than she pretends to be."

"But I'm young," Bekky said.

"And I'm not?" Lizzy asked. You're so well-read, Bek."

Tom climbed over the back of the wagon's front seat and sat down with Bekky and Lizzy.

"Okay," Lizzy said, "ask all those questions I know you've got bottled up."

"Well," Tom said, waving his arms to indicate the countryside, "why is the Earth so agrarian? Why in fifteen centuries haven't you regained the high level of technology Earth had before the Final War?"

"What?" Bekky asked, totally confused.

"Oh, my," Lizzy said. "I think we disagree, Tom, bout what constitutes technology. Let alone *high* technology."

"First of all, horses," Tom said. "No automobiles. Low-tech transportation."

"Horses," Lizzy said, "are the most pleasant type of transportation. With no need of automobiles, we don't have to use tons of steel—after mining more tons of iron ore—to make them in a gigantic manufacturing process, releasing much-too-much CO_2 into the atmosphere. And we don't need to use refined petroleum —"

"Petroleum must be drilled out the ground, or the seabed," Bekky added. Removal and accidental spillage of crude oil is disastrous for the environment "And besides, the Earth has almost completely run out of it."

"What?" Tom asked.

"Petroleum," Bekky answered. "Thank the Goddess," she mumbled quietly.

"Horses are beautiful living animals who require lots of green pasturage," Lizzy said. "Rather than covering the land with huge slabs of reinforced concrete for automobiles; horses turn grass and grain into fertilizer," she continued, "which smells better than burnt petroleum, and . . . and why wouldn't a sensible *civilized* people prefer horses for transportation rather than smelly, dead, dangerous automobiles? Horses are interesting, intelligent animals, and fun to take care of."

"Aye," Bekky added.

They were traveling east on K-96 — slowly, comfortably, listening to the rhythmic clop, clop of the horses hooves against the asphalt of the road — to visit some of their closest neighbors. The next stop was Guindilla Farm just cater-corner to the east across K-96 from Grasshopper Farm. The farmers there specialized in raising llamas for their soft wool, plus they devoted much acreage to growing wheat, amaranth, barley, and oats for the county bread bakery in Dighton. The crew from Yellowood traded gallons of milk, rounds of cheese, several dozen chicken eggs, a bag of horse manure, and tubs of butter for assorted bags of grain and bales of hay to feed their cows, chickens, and horses.

The shipmates of Guindilla spoke Spanish among themselves, and had done so from their founding nearly thirteen centuries before by 'immigrants' from the area in South America formerly known as Venezuela. They prided themselves on the great variety of hot peppers they cultivated in their large, tropically heated, geodesic-domed — EnergyScreened in the winter — tropical-garden. Food-cord Bekky insisted the Yellowood crew take along a variety of those peppers in small bags.

▼

"Sheldon, thanks for asking me along today," Tom said. "All this food sharing is fascinating to an Anthropologist."

"That's right. You share that interest with Lizzy, don't you?" Bekky remarked.

"Yep," he said, smiling at Lizzy.

"I'm hoping your Anthropological interest in Earth-culture is helping you adjust to never returning to Faraday," Sheldon said, turning around to face the second seat. The horses kept clopping along, not needing direction to stay on K-96 as it twisted and turned slightly, heading east.

"Well . . . all right. I suppose I *am* the luckiest exile in history, even if you—oops! I should say '*yall*' for the plural 'you', shouldn't I?—if *yall* do slip insects into my food!" Tom said. "I really can't understand how *yall* do it without money."

"Money is alien to us," Lizzy said. "But I realize from my reading of Anthropology how important money was to Earth's culture before the Final War. It's as if *money* were an actual *thing*, that it had a reality, an important existence of its own, aside from its supposed use as a way of keeping track of resources."

"We just share," Bekky remarked.

"That's right," Lizzy said." What we need to keep track of is that no human being (or companion animal) on this planet will ever again starve," Lizzy said. "We're all descended from rural people who survived the Final War because they weren't living in cities or suburbia. That's why our ancestors after the *Final War* decided to organize the Earth using farms. All children — however they choose to contribute to society as adults — are raised on farms, so all children are loved, given useful work to suit their abilities and interests, and are fed the amount of fiber, complex sugars, protein, vitamins, minerals, and *caring* they need to grow up healthy, strong, and *not* alienated."

"I know, Tom said. "Letting kids feel alienated, in any way, is bad for society as a whole."

"Most of us are farmers," Lizzy said, "like the folks at Yellowood or Grasshopper Farms, and we share the produce of our farms, sharing our local resources, as Poor people always did, in Solidarity —before the Final War — to survive together in Capitalism. Poor people didn't have much money — didn't have much of that symbol of the organizing of resources, didn't have much of that magical stuff — *money* — with its own reality. At that time in history, rich people, the Elites, could contrive to accumulate money and thus deprive a whole segment of the human species — Poor people — of the necessary resources needed by them and their children to survive. Seemed to me, in my reading of the Anthropology of the Earth before the Final War, that all money ever benefitted was rich people, the selfish, greedy Elites, whose very existence as a super-privileged class was based on, rested on, huge numbers of Poor people —"

"The Elites and their lackeys always blamed the Poor for their own oppression, for not having enough money to survive. . . ." Bekky chimed in.

"Aye. Blame the victim," Lizzie said.

▼

They stopped briefly at Fisher farm to trade cheese for fish.

"Back to technology," Tom said when they were again on the road. "Why hasn't your — excuse me, yall's — culture developed any newer technology? I know things like automatic dishwashers were invented before the Final War —"

"Haven't you heard anyone mention *stay*glass?" Lizzy snapped.

"Glass as unbreakable as steel. Extremely useful. All our windows, and our glass containers, are made of *stay*glass. Isn't that high tech enough for you?"

"Uh—"

"And '*stasis*'," Lizzy said. "Putting Entropy on hold. Doesn't require lots of steel or large amounts of refined petroleum, but the creation of our portable stasis-cupboards and stasis-egg-boxes *is* high tech."

"And we've eliminated most disease organisms from the earth," Bekky said. "From malaria to syphilis and AIDS, from smallpox, to salmonella, to yersinia. . . .'"

"Except for the so-called 'common cold', which is caused by a spectrum of viruses —" Lizzy said, "And most people these days are genetically-immune to it. Our BirthHouses have been selecting for that immunity for over fourteen hundred years, since it first appeared, as a rare beneficial mutation, in someone's genome. So now, almost everybody has the immunity."

"Or various kinds of viral-flu, which our healers can easily treat . . ." Sheldon said.

"And almost no one carries the genetic code for male-pattern baldness," Sheldon added.

"And mastitis in cows and nanny-goats," Becky said. "That's recently gotten worse, according to Nan, our county vet, but our scientists are working on it. . . . "They think it's caused by a new, recently-mutated, formerly-benign bacteria."

"Okay, okay," Tom said. "What about spaceflight? Faraday is way ahead of you there."

"You mean besides Weapons of War?" Lizzy asked, sneering at him.

"Uh, yeah. Okay."

"Over the seventy-four or so generations since the triumph of the Earth Recovery Movement," Bekky said, "the Space Collective has not been able to get a global consensus to use any of our precious, limited resources to do anything in space besides maintain our communication satellites."

"Right now," Lizzy said, "there's a push on to move some of our dirtiest manufacturing to Luna, because our Moon doesn't have an atmosphere to ruin, and smokestack-scrubbers—which we need here on Earth—are expensive in resources, and in carbon-footprint, to manufacture."

"I think I'm going to vote for it, at the next global eMeet this coming January," Bekky said.

"Me too," Sheldon said from his front seat.

▼

Still on K-96, down the road from Fisher Farm, was New Pearl Farm. "Was founded less than a hundred years before now by some people who lived—and experimentally gardened—on Pearl Street in Dighton Village," Sheldon told Tom. "New Pearl's fields grow ordinary grains for the Dighton Bread Bakery, and a special variety of potatoes as a staple crop to trade with their neighbors."

"Want to take home a sack of tasty New Pearl Potatoes for my planned meals," Bekky said.

Yellowood left New Pearl Farm some various vegetables and berries, and two bags of horse manure. When Tom asked why they didn't leave that farm any milk, Sheldon told him New Pearl had a supply of milk, butter, cheese, and eggs from other neighbors close by.

Heritage Farm was further east, approaching the border with Ness County. It varied from all the other Farms in the area because it attempted to function as an old fashioned '*family farm*', as they were thought to have existed at the end of the Elite Ages, just before the Final War. They were supposedly self sufficient, an experimental endeavor, not needing full Solidarity with their neighbors, having a few goats to supply their own milk, two steers to pull their plow and for manure production, chickens for eggs, a large vegetable garden, bee hives, fruit trees, and a small wheat field so they could make their own bread.

Their Earthship® provided them with shelter, vegetables, and berries year round, with electricity from the photovoltaics and the windmills. They had a large artificial pond under an all-weather dome, stocked with fish and ducks, but they had no horses, considering them to be a luxury.

Of course, they would actually need Solidarity occasionally with their neighbors to replace their steers (which, being castrated, could not reproduce), or to rebuild their Earthship when necessary. But everyone thought the experiment interesting, proving how much better it was to organize civilization in Solidarity on the county—or village-and-surroundings—level, rather than with a small group such as a 'family', as was done in the Elite Ages when the male-dominated nuclear family was considered to be the organizing unit of all civilization. After the *Final War*, the left-behind survivors had organized around their villages and their BirthHouses, believing the well-known African saying, '*It takes a village to raise a child*', was very true.

The Yellowood shipmates traded bananas, cow cheese, and butter with the Heritage '*family*' for three dozen duck eggs, and they accepted an invitation to lunch.

Bekky gloried in a meal she hadn't had to prepare, and praised Heritage Farm's food-cord for his cooking. They put their heads together about recipes.

Sheldon asked, and then went out to the geodesic-domed-over pond with two of the children to feed the ducks.

Learning that the Yellowood and Heritage Crews didn't really know each other, Tom marveled at how well they got along, like relatives who hadn't visited each other in a while, he thought. He had never seen anything like it. "How can you be so friendly with people who are strangers?" he asked Lizzy.

"We ain't strangers," she replied. "We're all human beings, People of the Earth, and we have farms in common. All grew up on farms, even if we ain't farmers as adults."

"Wow! No strangers. That's fantastic." Tom said.

Back on the wagon, he asked, "But still, I don't understand why your culture doesn't work to benefit everyone — as you do, apparently, with everything — benefit everyone with higher technology, an ability you deserve as civilized human beings."

"What higher technology do you think we need?" Lizzy asked with ill-concealed irritation.

"Machines to help with the work," Tom said, "like tractors, instead of planting by hand, as you know I've helped to do."

"Generally speaking," Lizzy answered, "gardens are best planted by hand. We *do* use tractors to plant and harvest fields of grain, or to maintain pastures for horses, cows, goats, or llamas, but not every Farm has a tractor. We trade them round. There's a syndic in Dighton stores and repairs the tractors, takes care of them. But some people prefer to use horses to plow fields. Varies."

"Oh."

"And as for other labor-saving devices, it depends on the labor,"

"What?"

"We've known for many centuries — from before the Final War, matter of fact — that people *need* to work with their hands, or they feel disconnected from the world and alienated. '*It is useless work that darkens the heart,*' as one great philosopher, *Ursula K. Le Guin*, once wrote."

"But —"

"You've seen our dishwasher?"

"Of course."

"Does the job better than washing dishes by hand, which is boring work, in my opinion, and you haven't seen our clothes washer, have you?"

"Uh, no."

"Clothes washers—powered easily, like the dishwashers, with electricity from our photovoltaic cells, or our windmills—are better than pounding clothes on rocks in a river, right? Or a washboard."

"Or pounding dishes on rocks," Bekky said. They all laughed. Tom lagged behind, needing a moment to realize Bekky was kidding.

"Then there's clothes dryers," Lizzy continued, "so that we only hang on lines those special clothes we think need the sun and the wind, outdoors.

"You see, Tom, we use machines—which we have to manufacture using steel made from iron ore pulled from deep in the Earth, or recycle from obsolete machines, and we have very few obsolete machines. . . .

"Mmm . . . We use machines sparingly," she continued, "to aide our human hands only when we need to. Machines don't overwhelm us, or rule us, or take over our bodies and become part of us, as was speculated a couple of centuries before the Final War. Certainly no one of us wanted to change into machines—think the term is cyborgs—especially after the Final War."

▼

Further east, just over the border into Ness County, near Beeler Village almost to the Carver Homestead Farm, they turned off at *TeroMagio Bieno* (Earth-Magic Farm), founded originally by some young people who had come to the area to teach *Esperanto* during the successful Earth Recovery Movement following the *Final War*. The *TeroMagio* shipmates—with their neighbors—had rebuilt their Earthship® only once, six centuries before, in the millennia and a half since their founding. (Yellowood Earthship® had been rebuilt twice since the late twenty-first century.)

They left vegetables and a few tubs of cow butter, and cow-cheese, but no milk. *TeroMagio Bieno* kept goats, farming enough naturally homogenized goats' milk to supply themselves as well as any newborn babies in the area who needed an easily digestible animal milk when there was unfortunately no available supply of human milk for them. Goats' milk—with smaller fat globules—was easier for human babies to digest than cows' milk.

Before turning around and heading westward for home, Sheldon and Bekky took Tom to see the small monument to George Washington Carver marking one corner of Carver Homestead Memorial Farm.

"Who was he?" Tom asked.

"Ness County's most famous Elite Era resident," Sheldon said. "Was born into slavery right before the USA's Civil War, in the nineteenth century, and was freed from slavery by the War. His former owners, the Carvers, people pale as you and Bekky" — (*she sneered and stuck her tongue out at him*) — "raised him and his younger brother as their own children. He was a gifted agricultural scientist, famous for inventing hundreds of things to do with sweet potatoes and peanuts, most notably peanut butter. And he was one of the first people in the area to advocate crop rotation. Oh, and . . . Bekky, can you add anything?"

"No, that's it for me," she said. "I'm not good at history. But I *do* love peanut butter. Love to cook with it too."

"Okay. Then let's go home," Sheldon said.

"Oh, yes," Tom cheered.

22

▼

THE STARSHIP

On *TeroOni* — once all the Faradayans, including Final Clones, were in cryo-freeze — a spaceplane docked bringing the spacer volunteers who were women or herms. The Earth*men*, even those who were homosexual, were delighted. Human society seemed to all of them healthier, vibrant, and more *real* when it was *not* one (or two)-gendered. (Or only one shade of melanin-colour.)

After the ecstatic hugging and spontaneous singing and dancing were done, they all sprawled in a large circle on the land to discuss their goals as a collective and the details of their work together. They spoke *Esperanto*, since they came from all over the Earth and there was such great variation in their ethnic languages.

One slim, mahogany-coloured woman stood up, microphone in hand, flanked by two nut-brown colleagues, one apparently male, the other probably herm. She addressed the circle, speaking *Esperanto* with an Arabic accent: "I'm Netanya Az Zahiriyah. These are Remy Beaumont and Dag Holyhead," she said, indicating her colleagues. "We're genetic Scientists, and we plan to spend our time on board researching a solution to the primary problem we face with the Faradayans."

Corazon Yen-Bai—having picked the red token in the immediate pre-meeting lottery—was temporary facilitator. She said, "Netanya, could you tell us a little bit more bout your research and its purpose?"

"Aye," Netanya said. "We know that long ago on Earth, during the Dinosaur Age, our pre-mammalian ancestors were infected by a retrovirus which invaded their reproductive cells, adding its viral

DNA to the inheritable genetic code of the animal. This insured the virus's existence for many generations while those small proto-mammals avoided genocidal predation by huge dinosaurs who were eventually wiped out by that asteroid strike sixty-five million years ago, leaving the Earth then free of gigantic reptilian predators on land, safer for the development of smaller mammalian life."

Several people raised their hands with questions.

"Now hang on," Netanya continued, "my preliminary remarks will be clear in a moment.

"Eventually" — she continued, after pausing to make sure she would not be interrupted — "as those pre-mammals further evolved, over many generations, that retrovirus DNA combined with other genetic material and helped create the mammalian placenta, which is a basic part of what being a mammal means. Something like that happened to the colonists on Faraday."

"What?" several people asked. Since they knew Faraday's reproductive problems were responsible for the Invasion they had just survived, they were all very interested.

"We know now that the inherent tendency to *xenophobia*, a disease really — which we conquered culturally in our post-Final-War society — was a very useful instinct when our ancestors were animals and needed, for the future of our species, to mate only with members of the same species and not any other semi-human animals round them at the time. . . .

"So an alien retrovirus, native to planet Faraday," she continued, "infected the early colonists and reinforced that ancient, outdated, anti-social, human tendency to xenophobia, that is, *fear and hatred of the 'stranger'*."

"Now we know what happened, what can we do bout it?" Corazon asked.

"We hope to create a nano-sized bio-particle," Dag Holyhead spoke up. "An artificial retrovirus which can invade the Faradayan humans' genome and negate the effects of the xenophobia-enhancing genetic material most Faradayans now apparently carry."

"A virus with a bacterial spore-coat, which we can spray over the planet from orbit," Remy Beaumont added, "thus potentially infecting the entire population."

"Against their wills!!!?" Elombe Caldwell barked. "That violates the basic ideals of our Anarkhist culture: no force against anyone's will, total freedom (in solidarity) for individuals, transparency of all applied science and technology —"

"The Faradayans tried to kill us all, kidnap women unlucky enough to be pale-skinned, and decimate our planet," Araminta Phelps snarled as she interrupted. She had medium-brown skin-colour and a fine cloud of relaxed black kinky hair crowning her head, surrounding her fine, chiseled, somewhat Semitic features. "We are still actually at war with them. Rapprochement giving us control of *TeroOni* is only a lull in the ongoing war which began with their Invasion of our planet —"

"The natural human tendency to Solidarity is easily derailed by *forcing* people, damaging both their ability to be egalitarian and to trust other human beings," Corazon Yen Bai said. In making the comment, she was stepping outside her role as facilitator, but no one really noticed. In their semi-Utopian, Anarkhist society, 'rules' and 'roles' were often side-stepped in favor of personal freedom.

"And, remember, the onset of their severe xenophobia happened to them against their wills, causing them to murder more than half their population," Leslie Sharyngol snapped. Zee was a lean, small-breasted, olive-skinned herm with nappy hair, wearing pale green lederhosen and a rainbow-striped T-shirt. "Those people are diseased," zee snarled. "We have lately experienced the terrible effects of their terminal, panicked thrashing-bout. Let's be realistic and admit the Faradayans would never consent to being 'cured' by us. They know nothing of solidarity, nor even of trusting other human beings."

▼

"So, we're agreed bout our ongoing bio-research and it's ultimate goal," Corazon the Facilitator said a half hour later, summing up the discussion thus far. "We have time for more talk. Does anyone have an idea what else this ad-hoc committee needs to plan for in our lives together on this starship?"

"We need to open-up the discussion to everyone on board, I think," Elombe said. "All the people who had to work today had no chance to share their ideas. Unfortunately, here on TeroOni we can't all take off work at once. A planet will keep running without constant, undivided, detailed attention from the passengers, but not a starship.

"The danger is," he continued, "if this committee takes upon itself the power to make decisions for everybody, then we are running the risk of forming hierarchy, of dividing ourselves up into separate groups with different amounts of social power, and that way leads to the death of Anarkhy, the ruination of Solidarity, and of our Freedom as individuals. I think preventing hierarchy and social-separation is the most important problem we have now among ourselves on this spaceship."

"I agree," said Morgan Cloudcroft, one of the recently arrived women. Her skin was a light-mahogany colour with many copper highlights, and her straight, shoulder-length, shiny-black hair was held back by a headband sporting an elegant grey and blue striped feather. "We *must* find a way for all of us to participate in important discussions, any ones we may want, possibly even while we're working."

"Aye," Remy Beaumont said. Zee also was wearing a headband with a feather. People even partially descended from the historic Indigenous population of North America, so called American 'Indians' or Native Americans, wore feathers — actual or representative — to mark themselves and show pride in their ancestry as the very first humans to colonize the North (or the South) American continent.

"Maybe we can make good use of the *Interkonsento / Centra* programming," Remy continued. "We have it on board, I hope? People could easily take part in discussions even while they are overseeing critical read outs."

"Good idea," Elombe said. "If we don't have the *Interkonsento / Centra* programming on board, we can easily get it via our ansible. We've already checked the ansible is working."

"Great!" Lucy LasCrucas said. She was a sepia-coloured woman wearing lots of turquoise jewelry, sitting very close beside Morgan. They were partners from the area formerly known as New Mexico. "We must remember to always watch ourselves so we don't slip stupidly into hierarchy," Lucy said.

"Aye," Elombe said. "But I must remind yall that since I was the first Earth person to come aboard this starship, *I am the Senior*, and thus the Captain of *TeroOni*. I expect everyone to be obsequious."

"Aye, aye," several of the committee members chanted, standing up and bowing facetiously to Elombe.

Remy Beaumont bowed in the opposite direction, away from Elombe, lowering hir trousers but not hir underwear, half-mooning him, which was the most modern custom. Everyone laughed, and the meeting of the first ad-hoc committee broke up amicably.

23

▼

PEASANT-EARTH

In autumn, when the heart-shaped leaves of the Quaking Aspen trees at Yellowood Farm turned yellow, Tom-&-Lizzy took one morning off—except for breakfast and Lizzy's early morning chores—and they went by horseback to the BirthHouse in Dighton Village for reproductive counseling. Tom was learning how to manage any amiable, well-trained horse.

Before the time he had committed Treason to the Invasion and had rescued Manda, Tom had been anticipating the Faradayans would succeed in their Invasion and once they returned to Faraday, would be reproducing once again in the old fashioned, natural, in-body manner of their ancestors. He was still leery of the Earth's reproduction procedures, as he dimly understood them, which he regarded as strange and voluntary, not a necessity, since Earth had plenty of healthy young women. And so he was feeling confused, generally grouchy, and somewhat alienated that morning.

▼

"Aren't yall afraid making reproduction an artificial process will endanger the species by our losing the ability to grow further human beings naturally? God's Plan, I think," Tom said.

"Meaning always inside women's bodies?" Lizzy asked. "With all the many dangers to the woman and the fetus that your version of 'God's plan' entails?"

Tom-&-Lizzy were in a small conference room in the Dighton

BirthHouse, seated at a small table, consulting with a Worker there (a birth-advocate) about their plans to make a baby together. The Worker, Vladimir Chilcoot-Vinton, was a male because Lizzy thought consulting with a male advocate would be more comfortable for Tom.

"Way we make babies now on Earth is not 'artificial', Tom," Vladimir said. "We have been able, since soon after the Final War, to scrutinize reproductive material so we can, by choice, pass on to our descendants the best genetics we have. Our culture developing that ability must be part of God's Plan, don't yuh think?

"At first," he continued, "we were most concerned bout eliminating genes damaged by severe radiation from the bombed cities. Since then, our BirthHouses have freed women — and everyone else — to absolutely choose when and with whom to reproduce. And for the last fifteen centuries, our skill at scientific gene-screening has given everyone a chance to make the best babies possible for them, with the most compatible and beautiful combination of genes from both donors.

"Aye," Lizzy said. "That's right!"

"So which of Tom-&-Lizzy's traits do we want the baby to have?" Vladimir asked.

"Skin colour like mine or darker," Lizzy said. She put her hand on Tom's arm. "So the child won't get burned skin like you do in the sun."

Tom nodded. He had cream soothing the bridge of his nose and his cheekbones. He hadn't worn any sun-cream (or a hat) when he was working outside at Yellowood Farm the day before. He wasn't used to being outside in direct sunlight for such a long stretch of time. He was too fair, as a blonde, to tan well. "Okay," he said. "Seems like a good idea."

"Will it activate your Faradayan xenophobia bout non-white people?" Lizzy asked.

"I think not," he said, leering softly at her, his eyes shining. He knew he was lucky that replicative fading had made him deficient in xenophobia. He had little unreasonable fear-of-different-humans to overcome. She grinned back at him.

"What might you want, Tom?" Vladimir asked.

"Eyes like Lizzy's," Tom said. "They're so attractive."

Lizzy was startled.

"You mean her epicanthic folds or her eye colour?" Vladimir asked.

"The folds," Tom answered.

"Epicanthic folds are an evolutionary cold adaptation," Vladimir said. "Originally found in people who lived in Asia, specially the north. Lizzy's are a result of Earth's great co-mingling of our human, so-called 'racial' traits — like Caucasian hairiness, African melanin-rich skin, the Asian epicanthic eye folds, the prominent noses of some Native American or Semitic people —the genetic mingling which occurred since the end of the Elite Era after the Final War. A result of our custom of everyone taking a YouthTrip and exploring the whole world when young.

"The somatic display of epicanthic folds is controlled by the gene's 'incomplete dominance'," Vladimir continued, "which works best when both parents have the eye folds. But we can select for various genetic potentiators and facial contours, and maybe swap some genes from one of Lizzy's unused chromosomes onto Tom's. I think we can do it. We'll run some computer models first. What else?"

"Tom's blue eyes," Lizzy said. Tom was flattered but not surprised. He came from a planetary culture where his blue eyes were considered most attractive, ahead of hazel, brown, or black, exceeded only by green. He began to relax to the idea of Earth's 'peculiar,' 'artificial' reproductive procedures.

"Well," Vladimir said, "eye colour is determined largely by the genetic inheritance of melanin and is thus closely aligned with skin colour. But we can fiddle with the potentiating genes and do it, I think. Blue eyes are a recessive trait. How bout green if we can't get blue with the amount of melanin we'll need for skin colour?" he asked Lizzy.

"Okay," she said. "But I'd prefer blue, if it'll work. Or turquoise."

"Great. Anything else?" Vladimir asked.

"An interest in science, of course," Tom said. "Is that genetic?"

"Aye," Vladimir said. "Multiple genes, of course, reinforced from both donors. You both have an interest in science, I understand."

"And farming," Lizzy said. We're all descended from farmers, of course, cept Tom. So maybe farming will be a trait in need of special choice also in our baby?"

"Let's take a look at yall's codes," Vladimir said, standing up and putting on his 3D goggles. Lizzy and Tom did also. The table and chairs sank into the floor of the conference room. Then the entire floor was a 3D stage.

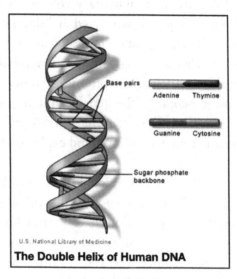

The Double Helix of Human DNA

the double helix

    They were surrounded by multi-colored representations of DNA double helices: Lizzy's sugar phosphate spiral backbones in deep pink, Tom's in royal blue, the base pairs in green, yellow, deep orange and red. Vladimir waved his hands, fingers flashing, and the colors whirled slowly around them. "There!" he said. "See those base pairs, in Lizzy's chromosome there? Right there." He pointed. "Those are the farming genes. *Far 14*, we call the grouping, although it's actually a lot more complicated than that, needing reinforcement from other gene complexes. Your tendencies to farming are strong, Lizzy, and backed up by potentiating code, see here? And here?"

    "Okay," Lizzy said. "That be enough, for the baby?"

    "Tom carries a smaller version of *Far 14* too," Vladimir said. "See here? But his potentiating code is different. I'm afraid he was destined to be a lousy soldier —"

    "Ha!" Tom yelped. "See?"

    "Aye," Lizzy said. "Manda was lucky it was you. So our baby will want to be a farmer?" she asked Vladimir.

"Uh, probably, but we also need scientists, researchers, teachers, and —"

"I want my children to be farmers!" Lizzy snapped.

"You know we never push children to chose a certain profession, Lizzy. Most want to be farmers, anyway. Was rural people survived the Final War. We're all inclined that way. Reason Earth has maybe a few more farms than we really need. You know you have to relax and let children be free. All our children, who ain't anyone's property, not even their genetic donors. Okay?"

"Aye, aye. Frack it," she said.

"Let me suggest . . . See here, and here. Combine those genes from each of you, and these potentiators, and yall's kid'll be a talented dancer, least more than most. Shall we?" Vladimir asked.

"Aye. Great," Lizzy said.

"Okay, I guess . . . Really?" Tom asked.

"Aye," Vladimir answered. "Will the child be a girl, a boy, or a herm?"

"Girl," Tom-&-Lizzy answered together. They looked at each other and smiled.

"We'll make a boy in a couple of years," Lizzy said.

"Sure," Tom said. Actually, he was feeling pretty good. A girl! He had never thought he would have a daughter. . . .

EPILOG

───────── ▼ ─────────

PEASANT-EARTH

More than three years after the Invasion, in December of 3686, Manda Dighton returned to Yellowood Farm from her *s*econd YouthTrip to visit with her old shipmates. She meant to stay long enough to dance with local African-&-Indigenous drums in the great Pagan celebrations of the Winter Solstice, which she remembered were enthusiastically celebrated in the winter-*in*-*active* grain-fields of Rosebud Farm in that area of Lane County.

Late morning, she disembarked from a typical solar-plane at Annabella Airstation on eleventh street on the western edge of Dighton Village. The landscape was dusted with a half-inch of snow and the air was crisp with cold. She was dressed warmly in thick-soled, fur-lined boots, dark-blue wool trousers over knitted silk 'long-johns', and two layers of cotton shirts with a wool sweater under her heavy woolen winter half-coat. Bob-&-Dillon were there to greet her. They had brought her favorite of the farm's horses, Alexander-the-Great, he of the warm brown eyes and the sleek dark-brown coat.

The horses were clothed in wide, warm woolen blankets under their saddles. Manda felt as though her heart would explode with happiness to see her Dads and her old friend Alex again.

"*Manda*," "Manda," "*Manda*," Bob-&-Dillon crooned, hugging her as she hugged her favorite horse. Alex whinnied happily.

"Oh, oh!" she cried. "I've missed you all so much!"

"Bekky has made a special lunch in your honor," Bob told her. "A grasshopper, potato, and cheese casserole, I think, with walnut bread."

"Oh, great!" Manda said. "I've missed Bekky's special breads."
"We'd better hurry," Dillon added.
"Okay."

▼

All over the Earth, it was always a special occasion for everyone
when a farm-child returned from their YouthTrip. Almost all the crew
of Yellowood Earthship® made sure to attend that special luncheon in
honor of Manda's visit.

Manda was seated at one end of the dining table opposite Bekky
Shields at the other end. As food-cord, Bekky always sat at the 'head'
of the table, nearest the kitchen. Bekky's pale-blond hair hung straight
over her ears and her eyebrows, obviously in need of a trim. Beside her
in a high chair, her three-year-old toddler — Titian-haired, dark-eyed
Hussein Dighton — fidgeted in his temporary captivity.

Manda's parents sat at her right hand, each of them grinning proudly
at her. Next to them, further down the table, was Jill Utica beside her
new partner, Haya Shoji, a new communard, a small woman nearing
middle age (58), with medium-brown skin-colour, sleek black hair down
to her shoulders, and black-eyes protected by epicanthic folds. She was a
root-vegetable expert and an experienced horse whisperer. Three years
before, Yellowood had advertised world-wide for someone to replace
Sheldon as the farm's horse whisperer. Jill-&-Haya — Manda was told
— had immediately fallen in love-at-first-sight.

Beside Haya sat Ora Dighton, 35 and still single. *She had always
said she was much too young to pair up*, Manda remembered. *Is she actually
asexual? Not interested in sex at all? Such people exist, I guess, but I sure don't
know how. . . .*

Next to Ora were Aisha McHenry and D'mitri Dauphin with their
first offspring, Belle Dighton, a dark-skinned, two-year-old herm in
a high chair between them. Mopping up the inevitable spills, it was
D'mitri's turn to oversee Belle enthusiastically spooning grasshopper
casserole into hir eager mouth.

Missing, Manda noticed regretfully, were Anelia and Edgardo
Dighton. They were again visiting the Intentional Jewish Community,

B'nai Khesed, where their gene-parents, Sheldon Rozel and Marsha Brownell, had decided to live for a while on Tikva Farm, so Sheldon could re-discover his Jewish roots. (Tikva Farm near Half-Acre Village in the ***B'nai Khesed*** community, far south by eastward from the Great Plains, in Marengo County,\ in the former Alabama, was where Manda had left Suzie's ovary when she visited.)

Sheldon had decided he wanted to live a more culturally-conventional Jewish life, maybe even enjoy practicing the religion full time, and Marsha had joined him. Their two children planned to fly back and forth between Tikva Farm and Yellowood Farm, so they could remain close to their parents while attending teen-school in the area where they were born. And Tikva Farm had ducks!

The kids would be returning to Yellowood Farm from ***B'nai Khesed*** community after a brief visit before their teen-school resumed after the Winter Solstice holiday. The Earth-custom was that children remained on the farm where they were raised, unless or until they relocated after their YouthTrips.

Also missing that day was George W.C. Healy, Bekky's partner, away helping Apiary-Blossom Farm with a minor engineering problem.

On Bekky's right hand — on the opposite side of the table from Bob-&-Dillon, Asa-&-D'mitri, Ora, Jill-&-Haya, and the two toddlers — was 14-year-old Bozena Dighton, Jill's daughter. She had grown taller and stouter in the three years since Manda had seen her. Next to her was Jameka Lunawanna, the farm's surviving retiree, then Lizzy Alamota and Tom Faraday, with their two-year-old, light-brown, auburn-haired, turquoise-eyed, a two-year-old girl in a high chair between them. She was competing with her agemate Belle Dighton across the table from her for number and range of spilled grasshopper casserole. Tom— who doted on his 'miracle' daughter, Mink Dighton—was working steadfastly to contain the spilled food, nowhere near as important a problem as they all were pretending.

Next to Tom-&-Lizzy and their child, at Manda's left hand, were Torrin Beeler and Russell Ravanna. It was obvious their relationship was just beginning. They leaned together and were both aglow with the enchantment of new love. Manda couldn't tell if Russell was a man or another herm like Torrin, but it didn't matter. Since Torrin, as a herm, had both an ovary and a testis in stasis in the Dighton BirthHouse —if they wanted to —the two could reproduce together easily, whether Russell was a man, a woman or another herm, without the special *chemical-hormonal-biological-assist* necessary when two men or two women wanted to directly combine their genetic material.

"Okay, Manda," Bob said. "Now is the time to give your old farm-family a full report of your second, and obviously successful, YouthTrip."

"Aye," Manda said. "Bekky, I've missed your special breads. This is terrific, as is the casserole." She wiggled a piece of walnut bread in demonstration.

"After the Solstice, I'll send you off with some loaves of bread to remember us by," Bekky said.

"Go on, Manda," Bob said.

"Sure, Dad. Well, first I went to Iceland, which is *much* colder and snowier — and abundantly less sunny — than here at Yellowood in the winter. So strange to see glaciers or mountains often visible instead of the big sky and the flat horizon like here in Lane County. They have bigger greenhouses there too. They're artificially lit since they have very long nights, and it rains a lot. But their seafood is delicious. Also they celebrate the coming of spring and increased sunlight much more enthusiastically than here in Lane County, although it never gets very warm. . . ."

"Good," Dillon said, "I knew you and . . . uh . . . you wanted to visit Iceland."

"Suzie," Manda said. I can talk bout her now. The pain is mostly gone. Some mindmenders I met in Iceland assisted me. Time has also helped, I think. Suzie will always be with me in my heart. I'll always be half a twin."

"So," Bob Beiler asked, "where did you go after Iceland?"

"Scandinavia. Beautiful landscapes. Intricate farming. Then, by accident, on the eastern Swedish peninsula, I boarded a ferry on a lark — with an attractive man I met on his holiday, Haukur Burgsvik — his skin is *so black* — and I embarked on Gotland Island, a beautiful place, and stayed. Their famous walled city, Visby, is in ruins under an EnergyShield, of course, but the island was always mostly rural, and is now so well-farmed, interlaced with ancient greenbelts, they have no need to import any food. And like Iceland, the seafood is great, of course.

"Similar to Dighton, Burgsvik Village is a hub for air-travel. After nosing around for a while, and talking to people, I finally decided to become a pilot with the AirTravel Syndic —"

"What?" Lizzy exclaimed. "You'll give up farming to fly all over the world?"

"I'll spend a lot of time at Black Goat Farm, ten miles south of Burgsvik, along the coast, where Haukur lives," she said, "so I won't lose my green thumb. You know, once a farmer, always a farmer. . . ."

"Well, well, my girl," Bob said. "A pilot. . . ." The other adults at the table, all surprised, conveyed their congratulations as Lizzy grumbled to herself.

"They let me fly part of the way to Dighton. I'll be a full-pilot in a couple of years. Uh . . . Haukur and I became partners," Manda continued, "and now we have a girl-fetus developing at the BirthHouse in Burgsvik Village —"

"So now Bob and I will have to travel to an island in the Baltic Sea to meet our grandchild, won't we?" Dillon said, interrupting. "Gotland. Never heard of the place."

"People always have to travel to meet their grandchildren, don't they?" Manda said. It's the way of the world. . . .

"Oh!" she continued, "and Rachel Rosenberg, Suzie's gene-mother—you remember I left Suzie's ovary in her care in the Half-Acre Village BirthHouse? Where they proved Suzie was Rachel's gene-daughter? — Rachel and her partner, Saul Berkman, used Suzie's ovary and his sperm to make a daughter for themselves, for Tikva Farm. You went to see her, didn't you?"

"Aye," Dillon said. "Very nice people, those Jews of Tikva Farm. And of course we'll go to your beautiful island to meet the Gotlanders and our second granddaughter. I'm so happy for you, Honey."

"She'll be decanted shortly after I return. But, Dads, yall wait til spring, you hear? Gotland is beautiful in the spring . . . late spring, in May. Will have a nice visit at Black Goat Farm. . . ."

"Tell us what it's like," Bob said.

"We have an Earthship®, horses, one cow, goats of course, sheep, and several Russ, the Gotland Pony, once unique to the island. They go back millennia before the Final War. It's thought the wild ponies of Gotland—the *Russ*—were first domesticated in the early Iron Age. Gorgeous creatures, all the spirit and the beauty of horses in a smaller package. They are very intelligent and have a notably pleasant temperament. They're great cart-ponies and excellent for children to ride. There's a herd of 300 wild Russ living on the wooded moors of Lojsta in the southern part of Gotland, free in that ancient greenspace. . . .

"Black Goat Farm also grows lots of dark-red raspberries, blackberries, dwarf black-cherry trees, delicious tomatoes, potatoes, plum trees, and so many flowers, even orchids, and roses. Lots of other vegetables. We fish a lot too."

"Okay!" Dillon and Bob said, almost in unison.

▼

After lunch, Manda, feeling somewhat 'zoned' by the long plane-trip across several time-zones, lounged in a comfortable over-stuffed chair next to a thick pillar radiating heat stored-up from the daytime sun. She briefly held Mink Dighton—Tom-&-Lizzy's two-year-old daughter—on her lap while the other adults quickly cleared the dining table.

Manda explained to the child who she was, a former shipmate of Yellowood Farm. Mink was obviously not interested. Then Manda put down the restless child who toddled on tippy-toes across the room to her father, who could always be counted-on to pick her up, swing her around, and set her on his shoulders. She squealed and grabbed his thick blonde hair for reins. Manda saw Tom's face twitch with a mixture of mild pain and great delight.

"Manda, it's wonderful to see you again, looking so happy and confident bout life," Aisha McHenry said, standing beside her chair.

"Thanks, Aisha. It's also great for me to see how well you and D'mitri did in making Belle. Zee seems like a brilliant arrow to shoot into the future. Do you think maybe someday the human race will have just one gender, the herm?"

"No. I think we'll always have three, or more maybe. Too many people love the traditional genders for them to go out of fashion, I think, eh? And if they do, our Legacy-Eggs-and-Sperms will always be there as a backup for tradition," Aisha said.

"Aye, I spose there'll always be folks like you and me," Manda said, "Tom-&-Lizzy, Bob-&-Dillon, and Jill, with mono-orientated sexuality — people attracted to only one gender — who'll want the traditional forms to survive in good number."

"We can hope! Eh?"

"Aye."

Aisha went over and hugged the thick pillar, soaking up its warmth. "Ah, Manda, I've got some work out in the barn with soil samples we'll want to be testing in the indoor garden this winter . . ."

"Of course. I don't want to keep you from your work. I'm on vacation, so I'll just sit here and enjoy the ambiance of my old GatherRoom," Manda said. She closed her eyes and thought about Suzie, remembering snippets from their childhood together at Yellowood. Then her thoughts drifted to Haukur . . . *what a wonderful lover he is* . . . and she dozed.

▼

"Manda, Manda," Dillon shook the young woman half-awake. "We've kept your old room ready for you. Come on to bed. It's late evening already."

"Uhh, umm . . . no, no. That's where I slept, my childhood with Suzie. Too many memories. You can give the room to someone else. Box up what's left of my books, papers, mmm, and photos, won't you? Airmail *mmm* to Black Goat Farm. Gave Bob the address. I'll stay in this chair out here. The GatherRoom'll be quiet at night, won't it?"

"Well, aye. I'll get you a pillow and a blanket. In the morning, you come and use our shower. Okay?"

"Okay. Uh, Dad?"

"What?"

"Thanks."

"Sure."

▼

At lunch on the day of the Winter Solstice, Manda told her old shipmates about having joined the new Neo-Pagan Movement which was quietly sweeping the planet, a symptom, non-joiners believed, of Earth having been traumatized by the Invasion.

"It was while Haukur and I were busy falling in love, staying in an AirTravel-Syndic hostel in Burgsvik near their residence and helping them part time with cooking for air-travelers," Manda said, answering Lizzy's question about when and how she had converted.

"But magic!" Lizzy snapped. *"Science* has helped us save the Earth, helped our ancestors save us and our beloved planet from the horrors of the Final War, and from the recent Invasion. How can so many intelligent people turn to magic?"

Manda sighed. She had thought the Solstice was the perfect time to tell her old childhood family about her excursion into a more spiritual life. *Lizzy is always irritable.* "You don't understand what we mean by magic."

"Ignoring scientific knowledge of the real laws of God, how the universe is actually, realistically put together —" Lizzy argued.

"That's not what we mean *at all,*" Manda protested.

"But, Manda —" Lizzy continued.

"People! Shipmates!" Jameka Lunawanna interrupted. "Let her speak! Please. Have some respect for the good sense, and the goodness, of someone who grew up among us. It's the very least we can do."

"Oh, sorry, Jameka, sorry," Lizzy mumbled.

"Sorry, Manda."

"Sorry," several others mumbled. Jameka spoke so seldom that, considering their automatic respect for her age — now 117, after her recent birthday — the shipmates of Yellowood always listened with respect whenever she *did* speak.

Manda said into the slightly embarrassed silence: "Magic, to us Neo-Pagans, means the wonderful, hard-to-scientifically-delineate connection between us humans, our helper and companion animals, the land, the crops, the wild animals, the seasonal rhythms and the ecology of our wonderful planet. Earth is the way it is today because we and our peasant-ancestors for the last fifteen centuries have been shepherding the Earth, taking care of it, celebrating it. . . .

"And we don't forget those peoples all over the Earth, during The Hard Times Under the Elites, who always cherished the Earth, even if it was dangerous or illegal. Like many Native Americans and their supporters did on this continent, at Standing Rock in the early twenty-first century, or earlier in history, people sneaking back into national parks at risk of their lives, after the US government had thrown the Native Americans out, because the Indigenous People felt it was their duty to shepherd the land, something white people didn't understand. Many ordinary people did their best to carefully guard the planet, especially in its rural and wilderness areas, which gave our ancestors after the Final War realistic resources to base the Recovery upon, for our healthy Anarkhist civilization, united in Solidarity."

"Manda, I —" Lizzy began.

Manda persisted, (now she was rolling), "For instance, that's why I came to dance the Northern Solstice celebrations with my Yellowood family this season, rather than stay with my lover and my new community to glorify this natural holiday of our planet. I wanted to celebrate the shortest-day here, at Yellowood Farm, where soo . . . ukh . . . Suzie and I were raised by wonderful people, and our neighbors, in tune with the Earth. Yall were magnificent humans who taught us love and caring, for ourselves, for each other, and the planet . . . ukh . . ."

She put her face in her hands, and fought tears, overwhelmed by her feelings of loss: of Suzie, of her childhood and its relative innocence. . . .

Dillon stood up and pulled her into his arms. She sobbed quietly against his chest. Bob came and put his arms around them both.

▼

Drums began to be heard outside—probably Torrin with two neighbors holding for hir, in a cradle, the big African-drum—**boom-boom**ing across the land. They were calling all the neighbors around the area to come out of their warm Earthships® and dance again, on that crispy-cold afternoon, in the fallow fields of Rosebud Farm. People would dance until early sundown, and then — humans chanting ancient melodies, accompanied by a complicated chorus of dog-barking, phox-crying, cow-mooing, horse-neighing, and cat-howling — they would even more noisily beg the sun to come back, to return and warm their planet again.

They were all modern people, and knew, of course, that Sol, the star of Earth, needed no human intervention to continue in its 'orbit' and return, first of all — as the Earth revolved — at sunrise the next morning. But their efforts, that yearly ritual — begging the sun to return — connected the humans (and their companion animals) to the planet and its natural rhythms, season by season, year by year, all over the Earth.

AFTERWARD

(about non-gendered pronouns)

English, like most languages on planet Earth, does not have an official gender-neutral, singular pronoun in common use. I understand that in the sixteenth century, "they and their" were somehow used for that purpose, but that use is grammatically incorrect today, although perhaps not in the vernacular. ("Is everyone ready for their ice-cream?")

The modern gender-fluid movement has given us a few suggestions for gender-neutral, singular pronouns. First of all, "they, them, their" for those questioning whether they are male or female, both or neither. If asked, I will use those words, but my ears cannot stop hearing *plural*. Also, recently created are "ze" and "hir." I prefer to write "zee," because the double "ee" rhymes with "she" and "he." "Hir" is a good compromise between "him" and "her," even if it does sound a lot like "her."

Since our modern culture is not yet accustomed to gender-fluid or gender-neutral ideas, almost any made-up pronouns will feel clumsy to everyone, even those who are not against the ideas of gender-fluidity or the stark reality that a minority of humans on planet Earth have always been born intersexed (and then surgically-*mutilated* as babies — before they are old enough to make an informed decision for themselves — to look like one of the traditional genders). In modern times, intersexed people are now organizing to stop that practice, so that intersexed people who come after them will not have their *original* genitals *mutilated* at birth until they can no longer feel sexual pleasure.

In my first novel, _Horned Humons,_ copyright 1984, (self-edited in 2014 into _A Unicorn of Kkhadee,_) I created the gender-neutral, singular pronoun "keh," with the possessive of "kez." They at least have the virtue of not sounding like any other pronouns in English.

When Ursula K. Le Guin wrote her break-out novel in 1969, *The Left Hand of Darkness*, and gave us her brilliant tale about humans truly androgynous, she did not complicate her story by inventing androgynous pronouns. Many of her readers were upset about that; but perhaps we can forgive one of the greatest writers who ever lived for her literary choices at that time (1969) in the history of Western society. *The Left Hand of Darkness* is still an unparalleled masterpiece.

about the spelling of Anarkhy

As a matter of taste, I have never liked the *official spelling* of "Anar<u>ch</u>y" or "anar<u>ch</u>ism." The word "anar<u>ch</u>ist" looks too much like the word anti-<u>Ch</u>rist. Since anarkhy has nothing to do with *the non-existent Satan*'s age-old War against <u>Ch</u>ristianity, I do not want theories of anarkhism to be associated in any way with that old, religious, so-called conflict.

Also, to a person who speaks only Ameriglish, as we do in the USA, "<u>ch</u>" is always pronounced as the "<u>ch</u>" in "<u>church</u>." "Kh" can be pronounced as it looks, with a throat-clearing sound or a raspy "k" as in words derived from German, like "te<u>ch</u>nology" or "ar<u>ch</u>itecture."

And considering the meaning of **Anarkhy**, how can there be an "*official*" spelling?

Thus I prefer to spell my favorite political idea as Anar<u>kh</u>ism, and my Hebrew name as Bra<u>kh</u>a. (The great Jewish comic Lewis Black says Hebrew is a language of phlegm.)

about people who helped

The book is dedicated to Kathryn Wilhelm, Managing Editor of Aqueduct Press, who instead of fobbing me off with a form-letter rejection, told me where the book needed work, and then looked at it again for me. And even though Aqueduct Press decided not to publish, she told me she really hoped I would be able to publish the book elsewhere. I am sure there is a special place in Heaven for a person of such kindness.

My personal editor, Kelly Ferjutz, recommended to me by my friend and bookbinder, Ellen Strong, was able to improve my writing style, although she had no knowledge of, nor particular liking for, the genre of science fiction.

Mae Genson, publishing consultant, my liaison with iUniverse, is a member of that most physically attractive of humanity's "races," the Philippine People. Her only failing was, I believe, that she flattered me much too much.

Also Samantha Anderson, also living in the Philippines, who — like Mae — worked in the middle of the night — since the Philippines are 12 hours different from Ohio, where I live — and whose job it was to coordinate the publication of many other books than just mine. So much better organized than I am, she was amazing.

the publishing process

Since it takes, I'm told, an average of twenty years, while continuously submitting one's manuscript over and over, to find a publisher to accept one's work; at the age of 77, I had to finally admit I did not have twenty years left.

So rather than spend money for postage and manuscript-printing, I decided to pay for "self"-publishing. After a long search, I settled on Gatekeeper Press, which did not work out. I do *NOT* recommend them to anyone.

Trolling through my own library at home, I came upon the novel of a friend of mine I hadn't read in years: *Rainbow Plantation Blues* by Robert L. Sheeley. I had helped him edit it, and he had gotten it "self"-published by iUniverse Publishing. Then I remembered I had had another friend who had published a few novels with iUniverse.

So I went with iUniverse for my own "self"-publishing. My experience with them has been positive — I think the cover art is amazingly good! — but we mis-communicated a bit about the formatting of the interior of the book, so that I am not completely happy with it. Being a new customer, I did not understand their procedures.

I will be publishing six more novels with iUniverse — should I live long enough! — and I look forward to the interior formatting being more to my liking.

Barbara G Louise
Cleveland Heights, Ohio
summer, 2021
(suffering in the heat of Climate Change)

Printed in the United States
by Baker & Taylor Publisher Services